The Ram

THE RAM STAM BOYS

English Schoolboy Novel by

CHRIS KENT

GLB PUBLISHERS   San Francisco

Second Edition
Copyright © 1999, 2004 by GLB Publishers
All rights reserved. Printed in the U.S.A.

No part of this publication may be reproduced or transmitted in any form or by any means, electronic or mechanical, including photocopy, recording or any information storage and retrieval system now known or to be invented, without permission in writing from the publisher, except by a reviewer who wishes to quote brief passages in connection with a review written for inclusion in a magazine, newspaper or broadcast.

Published in the United States by
GLB Publishers
P.O. Box 78212, San Francisco, CA 94107 USA

Cover by W. L. Warner

This is a work of fiction. Names, characters, places, and incidents are either the products of the author's imagination or are used fictitiously, and any resemblance to actual persons, living or dead, events, or locales is entirely coincidental.

Library of Congress Control Number

2004107336

ISBN   1-879194-52-X

First printing in Sept., 2004
10 9 8 7 6 5 4 3 2 1

Chapter 1

"Guy! Guy, darling, hurry up or you'll be late!"

I groaned and rolled on to my right side. Typical! My cock was hot, hard and throbbing in my right hand, middle finger of my left lodged in my anus; naked boys dived and swam in the cesspool of my mind—and my mother was calling up the stairs. For a few seconds I deliberated whether to pound my meat to orgasm anyway. Nope. The magic was gone. Save it for later in the day. It might be the only thing that made getting up worthwhile.

For the umpteenth time that holiday I wondered whether the pittance I made was worth the effort of getting up at five every morning. Assistant milkman was a title I could live without. Then I reminded myself what the money was for. That cheered me up a lot. It did nothing for my dick which lay semi-tumescent between my fingers and thumb. I gave it a few squeezes as crumbs of comfort then swung myself sleepily out of bed. I rubbed my eyes; it was awfully bright for the crack of dawn, and the birds had given up their demented dawn chorus a bit early.

The fog of sleep vanished as I remembered the date: September 10th! Back to school! Hence the extra two hours sleep. I grabbed my alarm. Seven not five o'clock! I'd picked up my last ten quid from Frank Summerhill the night before. Today it was into the monkey suit and back to school. The phrase had always had a horrid ring in my ear; at fifteen years old it sounded like a death knell. Still, it was a new term and a new year, and the place would be abounding with fresh meat. My cock stirred again. Down, boy, down, I say. I was going back to school but I was taking with me the guitar that all those early mornings had bought.

"Are you coming or not?" yelled mom.

"Fat chance," I thought, releasing my prick.

"On my way!" I yelled.

I scrambled out of my boxer shorts and paused for a moment in front of the wardrobe mirror. Not bad. Not bad at all. Fifteen. Just under six foot. No, not my cock. Legs that went on forever. Big cock. Big balls. Mind you, my procreative equipment was in a state of semi-tumescence, but it was big enough to titillate the shit out of the juniors in showers, so I'd nothing to complain about. Thick black curly hair. On my pubes as well as my head. And in my armpits. But nothing on my chest, as yet. That was a bit weird. I had lots of hair everywhere else but none on my chest. Big nipples though. Bigger when aroused. I was among the sixty per cent of men who have arousable nipples. Not many people know that. You do, now. There were a couple of hairs around my nipples. I tweaked them out. Ouch! Fucking ouch!

I peered at my face. Yes, I'm a little short-sighted, but only a little. A nice face, a trustworthy face. "There's no art to find the mind's construction in the face." King Duncan said that, and look what happened to him. Big eyes, thick eyelashes. But not too girlish. Nose too strong for that. Nice teeth, shiny, white, even teeth (thanks, mum - though I hated the fucking brace while I wore it. Have you ever tried getting some pubic hair out of...? Stop digressing. You didn't have time to finish your wank, so you definitely do not have time to digress. Get on with it.) Good, strong jawline. Well-defined cheekbones. A dimple (well, almost). I've got dimples in my ass. Look, if I bend over and... (Get on with it!) Back to the bod. That's a swimmer's body. Broad shoulders. Sweet pecs. Fuckin' hate swimming, but I don't mind having the body.

"Guy!"

I threw myself into my clothes—it felt funny having shoes on again—and bounced downstairs. Matthew was half-way through his breakfast; Jeremy was just starting. Pen portraits coming up. Matthew and Jeremy, my brothers, pains in the ass both. They'd gone back to school a week earlier, state school, and had to leave the house by 8.20 to get there on time. Matthew's 12, Jeremy's 11. They're both brighter than me (okay, brighter than I, for the pedants), so they'll probably win scholarships and follow in my footsteps. But not yet, not yet. Cute little buggers though. Mini versions of me, I suppose. And of Dad, I suppose, but we had to take mum's word for that.

"Guy, can I see your guitar before you pack it up? You did get it yesterday, didn't you?" Jeremy was in bed by the time I'd got home last night.

"Fuck off."

"Guy! Mind 'les crudities'!"

"Sorry, Mum. Okay, squirt. Finish your puffs (Sugar Puffs), then go and get it. It's on my trunk in the bedroom. Handle with care. As Groucho would say, it's F-R-A-G-I-L-E, fragily. And keep your fingers off my plectrum."

"Don't your masters object to your group rehearsing? The teachers at our school hate pop music." This came from Jeremy who was chewing a sausage like it was a Sixth Former's dick. Did my brother have talents in that direction?

"That's the difference between a pleb school like yours and a patrician institute like ours," quoth I. "Our masters are tolerant, creative, imaginative..."

"A bunch of wankers," concluded Matty.

"Matthew!"

"Sorry, Mum."

"You got it in one." That came from me. "Anyway, Tony fixed that. Tony can usually get what he wants. After all, he's in the Sixth, he's captain of rugger, captain of cricket, and his father owns the place. Even the masters listen to what ol' Tone says."

"Oh, Tony, Tony!" bleated Matthew, mimicking my

sycophantic whine to a T. "I'm sick of hearing about the wonderful Tony and that wonder horse of his. You'd think the sun shone out of his you-know-what." (My little brother wasn't far wrong.) "Thank goodness Tony Honeyman will have left Abertay before I get there next September."

"If you get there next September, you little fart," I retorted, stung by this unfair criticism of my hero who had not only explained to me the theory of fellatio but had introduced me to its practice during my first week at Abertay. I licked my lips at the memory. Down by the lake. I'd squatted against an elderberry tree, Tony's colt Ponyboy grazing a few yards away, while Tony fucked my mouth. He was gentle, at first. Then he'd really given it to me, holding me by the ears and pulling me backwards and forwards onto his prick. Even at fourteen Tony was a real mouthful. I still remembered the taste. Tony'd been eating lots of garlic before inviting me for a stroll by the lake—"to see the ducks." For the next few months, I wondered why all the boys didn't taste like garlic sausage, and where all the fucking ducks had gone.

"Now, boys, don't quarrel," broke in Mum from behind her Guardian. "It's just your hormones." Mum spent quite a bit of time pouring oil on troubled waters these days. It was a sore point with Matty and Jeremy that I had longer holidays than them. It was hardly my fault. "Matthew will pass for Abertay this September, Jeremy next, then we'll all have the same holidays again."

"That's right, Mum!" ejaculated Jeremy, spitting out several sugary puffs in his excitement. "We'll all go to Abertay and you'll be alone. Can I go and get Guy's guitar now?"

I snatched a look at Mum to see if she'd been hurt by this rather tactless remark. I had the uneasy feeling that we—or rather I, as the eldest male left at home, father having been posted to Thailand—did not give her the thought and care she deserved. In fact, my father observed Oscar Wilde's advice to the extreme. Not only was he neither seen nor heard, he was rarely if ever here. (We'd studied *An Ideal Husband* in the summer term, and I had a personal interest in all things Wildean.) Mum did so much for us, practically bringing us up single-handed while the Diplomatic Service shuttled my father to postings around the globe. There was no doubt; we were her hand-reared boys.

Mum gave us her Mona Lisa (smile). "I shan't mind, as long as my three boys turn out a credit to me and to their daddy. I wonder what Derek is doing this very minute." My parents' marriage would not have survived the answer to that question. Daddy was in fact lying naked on a bed in Phuket while two small Thai boys, equally naked, serviced his needs, one at each end, in much the same way as the British Diplomatic Service was fucking someone somewhere all over the globe. (How I came to know this will be revealed anon.)

"I know how glad…" Ah, she was still speaking, "…Daddy will be to hear how well everyone is doing. I don't think we could give him a better Christmas present than success all round." My mother actually spoke like that. She looked nothing like the Mona Lisa, but she spoke like that.

Further conversation was prevented by the return of Jeremy with my gorgeous new guitar. He and Matty took turns strumming it until it was time for mother to pack them off to St Michael's, a school which rumour had it was actually sponsored by Marks & Spencers, owing to a misunderstanding of what was to be found in the boys' underpants. Half an hour later, my taxi arrived to take me to the station for my journey westwards to the edge of the Suffolk border where I was to begin my Third Year.

Chapter 2

I settled down in a compartment and finished the final chapter of Jane Austen's *Mansfield Park*, part of my summer reading assignment. I'd started off with high hopes when I'd come across the sentence which read: "I'm going to make my little fanny feel as she's never felt before." High hopes of steamy sex evaporated as I discovered that 'fanny' should have been capitalized, the novel quickly turning into the typical over-rated Austen 'much ado about nothing'.

Give me Dickens any day. In 'Martin Chuzzlewit' I'd found: "She touched his organ, and from that bright epoch, even it, the old companion of his happiest hours, incapable as he had thought of elevation, began a new and deified existence." I wondered if Dickens had been pulling his readers' legs; he nearly had me pulling my plonker.

The Abertay cap with its purple and gold stripes was easy to spot. When I looked out of the carriage window at Cambridge, I spotted a likely lad, a stranger to me, standing only a few yards from my door. "Oi, young 'un," I called in true Abertay fashion, "Get in here if you're on your own." In real life, that is to say, anywhere at anytime outside school, we would never use language like that, but public schools, even as minor as ours, are a world apart and have their peculiar traditions.

The boy, obviously new, shouted, "Right ho. Just coming." He turned to say his good-byes to an elderly crone who came scuttling along the platform bearing a brown paper bag. She clutched the unfortunate child to her scrawny bosom and planted a wet smackeroonie on his left cheek. Lucky cheek! Selfish old bitch! The boy, blushing attractively, heaved her away, calling, "Thanks, Aunt Martha. I'll be quite all right now." He threw his bag into the carriage. "Here's a chap who's going to Abertay. He'll see me all right. Bye. I'll write in a day or two." Too puffed to pant, he threw himself on the seat opposite me as the train pulled out of Cambridge.

My previous traveling companions—a pregnant lady, a foul-smelling vicar (incense—High Anglican), and a Doberman Pincher—had decanted themselves at Bury St Edmunds. My companion and I had the compartment to ourselves. For a minute or so, the boy and I studied each other in silence. The newcomer, despite my earlier impression, was about my own age. Small, but perfectly formed as far as I could tell with his clothes on, very tanned, hair bleached blond by the sun. His tan made his blue eyes sparkle as if he'd been smoking one of those banned substances we'd been warned about in Personal & Social Education.

When he caught his breath, he introduced himself. "I'm so glad you saw me. Are you just starting at Abertay, too?"

"No, I've been there for three years," I said, slightly huffily. "My name is Tilson—Guy Tilson. Third Year."

"Parker—Peter. Peter Parker," he said redundantly. "Going into Third Year, too. I've lived in South America most of my life—my parents are missionaries out there…" I couldn't keep the smile from my face. Peter sighed. "I know, you're wondering if they do it in the missionary position. Fact is, I don't know. Haven't asked them, haven't seen them." A sense of humour. That augured well for our relationship. (He was strikingly good-looking, which was the main thing.) "They thought I should come home, finish my education in the UK. Uncle Johnny fixed up Abertay for me. An old boy and all that. Still, I'm glad I've met you. Don't much like traveling alone. But then again, this is England. Much safer." I wondered whether Peter was always this garrulous. Probably just nerves.

"Much safer than what?" I probed.

Peter blushed. "Well, you know. Good-looking young English boy, traveling alone, foreign country and all that. I had to do a lot of it."

"Fighting them off, were you?" I asked the question with a friendly laugh. "Not surprised. You are good-looking chap."

Peter responded with surprising confidence. "Thanks, Guy. I may call you Guy? Didn't actually have to fight them off, but had to run on a couple of occasions." I was dying to hear about those occasions, but I was a little preoccupied.

This train, same time, last year. Wonder if it was the same carriage. Good-looking bloke. In his twenties. Offered me sweets. I always accept sweets from strangers. Asked about me, about the school. I told him a pack of lies. I always tell strangers a pack of lies. Makes me seem far more interesting, at least to me. Offered me five quid. What the hell did he think I was? Offered me ten quid. That was better. But I wouldn't touch him. Nope, it was my needs or nothing.

Between Bury St Edmunds and Cambridge I stood at the window. I leaned out of the carriage. I know. Naughty, naughty. But this was the Norwich-Cambridge Line. The chances of meeting another train coming in the opposite direction were slightly better than me getting pregnant, but only slightly. I stood at the window, leaning out, sucking on his Polos. He leaned against me, crotch to bum, my bum, his crotch, slid his hand round me, into my flies, whipped me out, tossed me off for twenty minutes. It's a long, slow journey, and I was in no hurry. He huffed and puffed behind me, whispering "sweet nuthin's" in my ear.

(Dear Reader, don't do it. Don't whisper "sweet nuthin's" to schoolboys in uniform, or out. We don't like them. We don't like affection and we don't like romance. We like sweets, money and getting tossed off for free. The rest is just piss in a high wind.)

I handed him my handkerchief when I was about to come. Like a gentleman, he did the honours. He wasn't so lucky. I could feel his prick riding up and down the crack in my bottom—I was fully trousered!—and, unable to control himself, he shot what seemed like a huge load in his underpants, if he was wearing underpants. That killed the romance. He was off like a shot. But he left me his mints along with the tenner, so I still rate him a gentleman.

"... 'bout the school?"

I must have missed something. "Sorry, Peter—I may call you, Peter?—I was a little preoccupied."

"I was asking you to tell me something about the school, about Abertay."

"Oh, Abertay. Well, let's see. Abertay. A grand place, small for a boarding school, about 200 boys. We probably have an easier and freer life than you get at the more famous schools. It's all a bit laid-back. Topping playing fields; we're jolly good at hockey. We usually do well against much bigger schools at hockey. Ponies, too. I mean, there are half a dozen ponies for trekking over the moor. Beats walking." (A poor attempt at humour but mine own.) Lots of hobbies, too. There's a fine workshop for woodwork and metalwork. Music room, grand piano. What else?" I racked my brain. "No fags, I'm afraid. Headmaster doesn't like fags."

Peter's eyes fell. He looked disturbed, almost distressed. I racked my brains. What had I said? "You're too old to be a fag anyway," I consoled him. Then the penny dropped, or rather the kitchen sink. I burst out laughing. "Do you know what fags are?" I asked. "Not the kind you smoke." Peter shook his head glumly.

"Peter," I said delicately. He looked at me from those huge blue eyes fringed incongruously by light brown eyelashes. "In school terms, fags are boys in First Year who 'do' for older boys. Do services, I mean. Make tea and toast, clean their boots, run their baths. That sort of thing. The Headmaster banned it two years ago. But it's nothing to do with sex—alas..." The 'alas' just slipped out.

Peter looked at me quizzically, then burst out laughing. "So fag doesn't mean gay or anything like that."

"No, it doesn't," I reassured him. "It doesn't even mean bum–chum." I think Peter was about to explore the possibilities of bum–chum when he glanced upwards. He eyed the unmistakable guitar case on the rack above my head.

"Does the school have an orchestra?"

"Well, no, not a proper one. A few of the chaps play things like the violin and the flute, and they have a string quartet, but I belong to a pop group." Peter's animated expression encouraged me to go on. "There were four of us last term. Tony Honeyman, who plays drums, two guitarists and me. I played an old banjo which we found in the music room. And I did most of the singing. But my voice has started to break so I won't be able to do the lead singing much longer. Brett, one of the guitarists has left. I'm hoping to take his place. That's my new guitar up there." I couldn't keep the note of pride out of my voice. "Cost me an arm and a leg. Worked my bum off all summer to raise the money."

Did I blush? I might have. If I hadn't exactly 'worked my bum off' to get the money, I'd certainly had my cock sucked often enough. The image of Frank Summerhill's head bobbing between my legs flashed on my inner eye. It became a daily ritual. After we'd delivered all the milk, Frank would drive the float up Penny Lane, glide silently to a halt and reach for me. I was erect by the time he slipped open my overalls, slipped between my legs and slipped my hard-on into his thirsty mouth. There was something satisfying about sitting in a milk float parked in the morning quiet of a country lane with only the birds watching Mr Summerhill's head bob-bob-bobbing over my straining groin. Every time his head came up, he looked like the cat that had got the cream as my spunk ran down his chin. He grinned like the Cheshire cat, too. Of course, I could have made all the money I needed in one go.

Just let him have my cherry. But I was saving that for somebody special, somebody I already had in mind.

"Tony Honeyman?"

"Excuse me?"

"I was asking if Tony Honeyman was any relation to Dr Honeyman, the Headmaster." That came from Peter.

"Tony's Dr Honeyman's son. He doesn't make a big deal of it." I chuckled. "Beyond getting his own way most of the time. But Tony's such a diplomat nobody seems to mind. Would you like to see my guitar?"

"May I?"

I nodded. Peter sprang up from his seat and reached for the case in the rack. The train jolted and he was abruptly thrown forward. I had no choice. I leaned forward and grabbed him by the hips. The train was taking a notorious bend and continued to jolt erratically along the tracks. I held on, Peter's crotch directly in my face. 'Nothing ventured, nothing gained' has always been my motto. I leaned my face into the fabric of his flannels, my nose, then my lips pressed directly into the meat of his groin. He smelled so good. Cinnamon and what was that? …yes, spice. The smell reminded me of Christmas. There was faint tang of something else, something equally nose-pleasing. Peter hung onto the rack. I deliberately ran my nose gently the length of his groin. There was a definite stirring.

The train straightened itself out. Peter pulled down the case and let himself fall back into his seat. His face was glowing. "That was really something," he croaked. "Yes, that's a notorious bend," I agreed. "No damage done, I hope."

"No, none at all," Peter flustered. "I'll be better prepared next time." We exchanged what I hoped were conspiratorial smiles and turned our attention to the beautiful instrument in his lap. Peter opened the case with some reverence and drew out my shiny new guitar. I relieved him of the case. "Do you play?" I asked.

"A bit," he replied. "There were several instruments at the mission station. We had quite a happy group for my father's meetings." Peter ran an experimental thumb over the strings, released and tightened a couple, then played several chords. I recognised the song immediately though I couldn't name it. An idea came to me in a flash, like a burning fart in a darkened dormitory. Maybe we could get Peter into the group in the place of Brett. It wouldn't be any good unless he could do lead vocals. In any case, it would be up to Tony to decide. "Sing a little," I suggested.

"…So if you really love me, come on and let it show…"

Unbelievable! Even though Peter sang just above a whisper, it was easy to hear what a beautiful voice he had. Perfect pitch. Exquisite tone. Unbroken voice, with an underlying huskiness that signified his voice would soon be as unreliable as my own.

"…I see your face before me as I lay on my bed…" I added a harmony just below Peter's lead line. I pitched my voice low; it was safer that way. Together we sang: "…It's written on the wind, it's everywhere I go, so if you really love me, come on and let it show, come on and let it show…" We let our voices die away together and sat looking at each other until Peter coughed and broke the silence.

"I thought you couldn't sing," he said. "That was beautiful, just beautiful."

"Yes," I laughed, "but I don't get through too many songs now without my voice leaping an octave in either direction. Totally unpredictable. Now you, my boy, have a voice, and play guitar really well, too. By the way, what is that song? I can't get it out of my head."

"'Love Is All Around'. By the Troggs."

"By the who?" I asked.

"No, not by The Who," said Peter. "By the Troggs. We

played them a lot at the mission. The Indians liked them. And I know most of their songs by…"

"Ah, I've got it," I interrupted. "Maybe it was originally done by the Troggs, but it's the version by 'Wet Wet Wet' that I know. It was all over the place a few months ago. It was from that film 'Four Fucks and a Shag'." Peter's blush reminded me he was a missionary boy, Troggs or no Troggs. "Anyway," I blundered on. "I hope you'll get interested in joining our group. With you around, we could really go places."

"Do you think so?" smiled Peter. I was relieved to see the animated expression back on his face. "I was hoping to get the chance to play some music."

"Of course, the final decision's Tony's," I hastened to add. "But I can't see him turning down a boy like you. I certainly wouldn't." The silence reminded me that it was my day to blunder. What the hell? I was signaling my interest in the boy before we got to school, putting my marker down, so to speak. If he didn't want to know, that was fine, disappointing but fine. I began to wonder what it would be like to share the missionary position with Peter. My growing erection warned me not to push my luck too far. Not yet anyway.

"It's Tony who plays the drums, isn't it?" said Peter. "Is there a set belonging to the school?"

"No, they're Tony's personal set," I said. "It's an absolutely super outfit. He got them a couple of years ago. Must have cost a king's ransom."

Peter gave me a quizzical look. "I thought all the boys of Abertay were the sons of indigent parents, widows or missionaries like my folk. Aunt Martha said the school was endowed by a Scottish millionaire, especially for boys like us."

"True," I laughed, "but Tony's the exception. His father's not only the Headmaster but he's the proprietor of the school, too." I went on to explain a bit about Tony and his family while Peter strummed my guitar gently. Finally the train pulled into Kennet, the sleepy little town about three miles away from the school. We had two options. We could wait for the school minibus which arrived on the hour every hour to ferry boys to the school, or we could call up a taxi. In the event, we didn't have to make the choice.

Chapter 3

A silver Rolls Royce came sighing up the road which led from Kennet to Abertay. It glided to a halt in front of us. A window slid silently down. Out of that window came a shock of raven-black hair. Tony Honeyman! He gave us his trademark grin. "Hop in, you two. I'll give you a lift to school. Look sharp. If my father finds I've got the car out, there'll be hell to pay. He thinks I'm out exercising Ponyboy."

We piled our cases into the trunk and slid onto the back seat. I clutched onto my guitar.

"Thanks, Tony. This is Peter. He's a new boy. Third Year. And has he got talent!"

Tony's response was a low wolf-whistle. We slid silently away. The Autumn Term had begun.

Not until the following Saturday afternoon did I have the chance to speak to Tony Honeyman about the group. He caught up as Peter and I were strolling to the playing fields for a game of hockey. Since we were in neither the same House nor the same Year as Tony, there weren't many opportunities for us to meet. The previous year most our meetings had taken place down at the stables where some of the boys, including Tony, kept their horses. I wasn't very interested in horses, but I was interested in big dicks, one in particular that I swallowed and sucked most Saturday afternoons. Not Ponyboy's, I hasten to add!

"Hello, young Tilson," said Tony, putting his hand on my shoulder, grinning cheerfully. "You and Tim and I will have to get together about the band, to see if we can find somebody to take Brett's place. Come along to the music room this evening after supper. Eight o'clock."

"Super, Tony. You remember Peter Parker. You gave us a lift from the station. He's one helluva guitarist. Shall I bring him along? He's got a great voice, too."

Tony gave Peter a long, lingering look that seemed to undress him where he stood. Not that Peter was wearing much. He had obviously outgrown his sports things. The shirt was short, the shorts were tight. The curve of his bum and the bulge in his shorts would have had him arrested, or at least molested, in any public place. The fresh air and Tony's look brought a blush to his cheeks; he positively glowed, his healthy tan looking as if it were backlit.

"All right," said Tony. "We've got to find someone. Who knows, Peter might do. Eight o'clock then." He strode off in the direction of the Sixth Form block that lay on the edge of Brinley Woods, some half a mile from the main buildings. I'd never penetrated the Sixth Form centre though I'd been penetrated orally on several occasions in the woods.

Peter and I strolled on, bound for the smaller playing fields where the Second XI were to have a good try-out. I noticed Peter was frowning. "Does Honeyman always give orders like that?"

"Well, of course. He's a Sixth Former; we're humble third years. I keep forgetting you've never been to a proper school before. When you get into the Sixth Form, you're lord of all you survey. You've been through ten years of the meat grinder, including prep school. You've earned the right to be a little arrogant."

Peter was unconvinced. "But some of them are different," he remarked. "That tall, red-haired chap—Ackerley, I think his name is—came into my room this morning. He needed a couple of boys to help him move his desk from the study he shared last year. He was pleasant and polite. He asked Greg (Peter's room mate) and me if we could lend a hand. According to your theory, he should have said, 'You and you! Move this desk for me,' and we would have had to jump to it whether we wanted to or not. After we helped him move the desk, he kept me back a minute. Asked who I was. Asked if I was settling in okay. He's even invited me for tea one afternoon this term. That's the way we should all be to each other, kind, caring, interested."

"Oh, Ackerley! I couldn't imagine him giving orders to anyone. Why on earth he has been made Head Boy I can't imagine. It should have been Tony Honeyman except that would have looked like nepotism. Ackerley'll never be able to keep order in a thousand years. Just wait and see. There are several chaps in the Fifth who are given to bullying a bit. I can't see Ackerley having much control over them—unless Tony gives him total backing."

We'd arrived at the playing field which put an end to that conversation for a bit, but it was intriguing to learn that Ackerley had invited Peter for tea. Ackerley was a bit of a dark horse for a red-head. Of course, it could all be entirely innocent, but with legs like Peter's I defied any red-blooded boy not to look at them and lust a little.

The hockey trials were serious. I'd already got a place in the Seconds, and I was delighted when Peter got a place, too. He wasn't that strong but he was quick and nimble, and he could run with the ball at pace. That's what I liked about the game. You didn't need the physique of the Incredible Hulk to play a creditable game, and you didn't have to be an uncouth, foul-mouthed lout; essential qualifications to become a rugger bugger. Delighted that Peter had got a place in the side, I was disappointed that he didn't come with the rest of us to the showers. He pleaded a headache and set off for the dorms, double rooms, which also had baths, one between each pair of rooms, for a long, quiet soak. This would have been my first chance to see Peter as Nature intended; and Nature intended the sight would be something all of us could enjoy.

"Catch you later then," I said, hurrying off to catch everyone else up. There were some jolly good-lookers in the

Seconds. The previous term showers had sometimes ended up in fun and frolics. With any luck, we'd start where we left off and go a good deal further. My dick began to bulge my shorts.

To beat the others to the showers, I cut through the junior block, strictly forbidden, but then, there wouldn't be anyone there on a late Saturday afternoon. I was passing the door of the first form-form room when I heard a squeal from inside. I paused and listened.

"Shut up, you little shit!" The deep, dark tones of Mark Harper's voice were instantly recognisable. "You just listen to me. You're supposed to be in the junior common room. Not wandering junior block. The only thing you could be here for is to nick what you can. Right?"

The higher, lighter tones of an unbroken voice pleaded in response. "No, honestly. I forgot my fountain pen this morning. I need it for Letters. I wouldn't touch anything. Honestly."

"Typical of the new First Year. Bunch of lying little shits." There was menace in Harper's voice. "I'm going to say I caught you going through everyone's desk. I'm Fifth Form. They'll believe me. You'll get canned, sent down in disgrace. Unless…" A lengthy silence punctured by sobs.

"Unless what?" came the younger voice. "Tell me what I can do. I can't get sent down. I just can't. It would kill mother. She's a widow, you know. Oh anything, anything…"

"Well, I suppose we could carry out the initiation ceremony," said Harper in tones of eminent good sense. "All First Years have to go through it. You could just do it now, and that would show you're an honest chap, a real Abertayer. But if I let you do it, you can't tell anyone. I really shouldn't let you off but you seem a good kid. What did you say your name was—Fletcher, isn't it? Well, Fletcher, your luck's in this afternoon. Just do what you have to do and be on your way.

Then we'll say no more about it."

It didn't take a genius to work out what Harper's 'initiation ceremony' involved. How far would he go? I nursed my erection, waiting and wondering. I remembered who Fletcher was. Michael Fletcher, a delicate-looking kid who'd stood on the touch line with some First Year chums watching the hockey trials.

"Oh, I couldn't, Harper, really I couldn't." There was a note of desperation in Michael Fletcher's voice now.

"Don't be silly," said Harper. "Get on your knees. There, that's it. Go on. Hold it. It won't bite you. That's it. Come on, toss me off. You know what that is, don't you? You're not that stupid. Yes, that's right. Hold me a bit tighter. Use your other hand. My balls, you idiot, play with my balls! Shit, that feels good. Faster, please. Come on, it won't break." There was a silence. I strained to listen. Yes, there it was. The old familiar sound of skin sliding over shaft. Set to a background of quiet breathing.

"Put your hand right under. Go on. Wait, I'll open my legs a bit. There. That's it. Go on, slip your finger up. Touch me there, yes, right there. You're learning, Fletcher. No, don't take your finger away. Push it in, right in. Faster with your hand, please." Skin slid over skin, soft over hard, velvet over steel. I slipped my hand down my shorts; I was wet—wet, wet, wet. I could feel it on my fingers if not on my toes.

"Initiation time." That was Harper's voice. I'm not sure what a chuckle sounds like, but I think I'd just heard one. "Come on. Open that pretty little mouth of yours. If you suck as well as you toss, you're going to be a real find."

"I can't," came Fletcher's teary reply. "I just can't. Please don't make me! I've never done anything like this before. Don't, please don't. It's big, it's just too big. I can't put it in my mouth, I just can't!" The treble voice sounded petrified.

"Suck it or get canned," was Harper's brutal reply. "And

consider yourself lucky. I could put you over that desk and shag your little arsehole. Believe me, that would hurt a lot more than sucking my dick. Now open wide and see what God gives you…"

That was blasphemy. That was going too far. I flung the door open and stalked in. Michael Fletcher was on his knees in front of Mark Harper. The bigger boy's trousers and underpants were at his knees. His bare midriff was in the younger boy's face. Fletcher was right. Harper did have a big cock, a big big cock. The smaller boy gripped it in one hand, his fingertips lost in the thick dark hair at the base of Harper's prick. Said penis looked swollen and angry. Foreskin pulled back. Pre-cum glistening.

The small boy turned on his knees and looked up at me. His mouth was open, wide open. What big eyes! What a pretty mouth! What delicate features! Such a boy deserved tender, affectionate first-time sex, not this brutal rape of his mouth by an uncaring bully.

Startled by the interruption, Harper released his hold on the boy's shoulders. Fletcher let go Harper's cock and scuttled across the floor towards me. I pulled him up by the shoulders. "Get out of here," I ordered. Fletcher darted away with a look of gratitude which would have melted my heart if I hadn't suddenly realised what I'd done. I'd thwarted a Fifth Year, and a very horny one at that, in the act of satisfying his lust with a remarkably good-looking squirt. I'd be furious myself if our roles were reversed.

Harper tucked his cock away with some aplomb and buttoned himself up.

"You're Tilson, aren't you?" he asked. It was not a genuine question. "One of Honeyman's bumchums. Well, let me tell you something, Tilson. I'm in the Fifth Form. Honeyman's in the Sixth. Next year he'll be gone. But I won't. And neither will you." He paused. He stepped past me. He turned. "Work it out for yourself." He strode off, his erection bulging his flannels. If he'd stayed, we might have negotiated a compromise.

I realised I was trembling. I'd made a real enemy. There was a tug at my sleeve. I turned. It was Fletcher. "Thank you, Tilson. Thank you. I don't know what I'd have done if you hadn't come in. I was going to bite him hard and run." I winced at the thought, then smiled.

"That's all right, squirt. You just tell me if you have any more trouble." At that moment, basking in the glow of Fletcher's admiration, I could have tackled anyone, anything. "What were you doing, wandering round the classrooms by yourself on a Saturday evening?"

"My name's Fletcher—Michael Fletcher." Perhaps he hadn't heard the question. "Mummy calls me Mike." His voice trembled a little as he mentioned his mother. "She's a widow. Daddy's dead. It was something he ate. I just wanted something from my desk. It was…it was…only a letter. I had it from her yesterday. I wanted to read it again."

Memories of my first few homesick days at Abertay came flooding back. "You'll soon feel happier," I said, and wrapped an arm around his shoulder. "It's a jolly good place, really. There aren't many rotten types like Harper and his pals. You just keep away from them. Now come on. We're going to be late for dinner, and I've got to take a shower." I ushered him out of the room, out of the building. As we crossed The Green in the gathering gloom, the boy looked up at me.

"Tilson, may I ask you something?"

"Of course."

His voice was trembling again. "It's about the initiation. When I have to do it, can I do it with you? I wouldn't mind that too much."

Was this child simple?

I looked down into those huge eyes. I know I should have

disabused him, should have explained that the 'initiation ceremony' was an invention, a piece of arrant nonsense. But there, in the dusk, he looked so helpless, so pitiful, so pretty, so willing, I couldn't bring myself to do it. This boy was placing his trust in me.

"I'll think about it, Mike. May I call you Mike?" His eyes sparkled like fireflies. "I'll think about it. I'll let you know. But keep it a secret. Harper shouldn't have told you anything about the initiation ceremony. So whatever you do, let's keep it a secret between ourselves."

"Oh, I will, I will," sighed Michael Fletcher, leaning his hot little body into mine.

"Tilson, you're a bastard, a real bastard," I sighed to myself, leaning my body into his.

I left Fletcher to join the pack of hungry boys converging on the dining room while I made my way to the showers. Ten minutes later I pushed my way among the ravenous hordes who fell like Assyrians on heaps of lamb chops.

Saturday evening supper was rowdy and informal with no teacher in charge. As soon as Peter and I'd finished we collected my guitar and made our way to the music room. We had the place to ourselves. I started taking the covers off Tony's drums. Peter went over to one of the pianos and began picking out a tune I vaguely recognised.

"What's that?" I asked.

"What? Oh, this." He added harmony. "It's a Negro spiritual. We used to sing it with a guitar accompaniment at the mission services."

"Not quite what we need for a pop group," I suggested.

"No?" smiled Peter. "What about this?" He speeded up the tempo, altered the rhythms and banged the keys. It was stunning. The G8 tune suddenly changed into a rock anthem, then slid into something else: 'Great Balls of Fire' by Jerry Lee Lewis.

"Hold on! I know that." I plugged my guitar into the amplifier and hit a few basic chords. The effect was tremendous. The room filled with echoing, crescendoing sounds. We were so absorbed we hardly noticed Tony and Tim's arrival until the drums picked up the rhythm and a second guitar added its booming bass.

The next hour was grand fun. We played half a dozen old favourites, some things Peter suggested, some with piano, some with vocals, some with Peter as lead singer, and a couple that I could still croak through. By the end of the session, sweat was pouring from all of us, and we'd discarded our shirts in the face of some intense central heating. It must have been quite a sight. Four teenage boys, stripped to the waist, sweat pouring down their torsos, hair matted with sweat, crashing their way through a string of rock numbers.

Peter's voice was better than mine had ever been. I was confident that Tony would be glad to give him a place in the group.

I was right. Tony was elated as I, though you could only guess it from his grin. It was wider than ever. "That's it, Parker, you're in. Welcome to The Ram Stam Boys."

Peter beamed his acceptance, then asked the obvious question. "Why do you call yourselves The Ram Stam Boys? It's a weird name for a rock group, don't you think?"

"It was Guy's idea," said Tony.

"We were looking for a name," I said. "We tried lots of things, nothing seemed right. Then I remembered what my grandfather calls me and brothers when we visit him in Scotland. He calls us his 'ram stam' boys. 'Ram-stam' means reckless, like tearaways. Grandad told us that Robert Burns, you know the Scottish chap who wrote 'Auld Lang Syne,' used the expression about himself and his mates. Apparently they were a right bunch of tearaways. Anyway, we thought it sounded really good. And it is original, don't you think?"

I was embarrassed that I'd had to explain in such detail, but there didn't seem to be a simpler way. Peter's verdict reassured me. "Brilliant. I'm delighted to be a Ram Stam Boy."

Grins all 'round.

As we packed up, Tony spotted a slight movement of the curtains near the door. He moved forward as quickly as cat and seized a small arm, dragging the accompanying body into the middle of the room. "I spy with my little eye, something beginning with..." Michael Fletcher!

"What the...?" Too late. My recognition of the squirt was obvious.

"Fletcher," I sighed, "What on earth are you doing here?" The terrified look was back on the child's face.

"I just wanted to say thank you, Tilson. Thanks again for..."

"For what?" broke in Tony Honeyman, turning Fletcher round so we could view him from all angles. "Bit young for the Ram Stams," he mused, "but we could make an exception."

I hurriedly broke in. "It was nothing, really. I helped Fletcher out this afternoon but it was nothing, really."

Fletcher's eyes shone. "Oh no, you practically saved my life," he blurted, then went on to describe this afternoon's adventure in terms that made me sound like Sir Galahad. Fortunately, the boy was no fool. He completely left out the sexual element and made it sound like a pure case of bullying. His story panted to an end. Tony released him. There was dark look, rarely seen on the face of the Headmaster's son.

"I've had just about enough of Harper and his bullies. They're going to get their come-uppance sooner rather than later. We don't carry tales in this school, but I promise you before I leave..." He let the sentence hang in the air. "Oh, let's leave all that stuff for the moment. Let's not spoil this evening's fun. Let's get the next session organised. Tuesday evening, same time, same place. We'll try and put together a provisional programme and get to work on it. But for now, it's fuck-you-and-leave-you time. Tim and I are off to the Sixth Form C.R. We'd ask you along, but you know how it is." We nodded. We knew. Tony turned to young Fletcher.

"Now, squirt, time to pay the admission fee for watching a great rock band in action. Finish tidying up here. Put out the lights. Lock the door, and hand the keys in at the Lodge. Think you can manage that?" Fletcher nodded enthusiastically. "Bye then, fellow Rammers," laughed Tony, and he and Tim were off, singing the two greatest lines in all of rock 'n' roll: "Awobopaloobop Alopbamboom!"

I turned to Peter. "Great. You're in." We whooped and shook hands on it. "By the way, my room mate's off for the weekend. Family wedding. Probably his mother. Only joking. Care to spend Saturday night in my room? We can discuss the music programme. Maybe come up with some good ideas."

"Thanks," said Peter. "I'd like that. But I may be a little late. I promised to have supper with Dr Moonie (the school chaplain). He used to be a missionary. Knows my father. Wants to catch up on the news. You know how it is."

"Fine," I said, thinking, "Randy old bastard." Not Peter. Dr Moonie. The chaplain was well named. Though there was no proof positive, a few of the juniors he coached for confirmation seemed to emerge from the sessions with a new perspective on the world. I suspected they got some of that perspective on their knees, or perhaps sitting on the good doctor's knees. I'd heard somewhere that a missionary is a person who teaches cannibals to say grace before they eat him; in Dr Moonie's case, he probably taught the juniors to say grace before he ate them, or at least had a good lick.

"Now, now, don't be a hypocrite," I tutted to myself. I suddenly remembered Fletcher. He was struggling, trying to get the wrong drum cover over the wrong drum. "Hey, squirt,"

I called. He turned. The exasperation on his face was fun. "Try measuring them first." Peter and I left him to it.

I saw Peter halfway to the chaplaincy. He begged me to accompany him. "Dr Moonie won't mind." I would. "Not my cup of tea. Go and enjoy yourself. I'll see you later. Don't be too late." Peter gave a wry smile, "I won't," and with a cheerful, under the circumstances, grin trotted away into the night.

Chapter 4

I was rather at a loose end. I tried some television in the common room; rubbish. I tried a little pool; couldn't concentrate. Tried a pillow fight in a junior dorm; juvenile.

To tell the truth, I was restless. Everything seemed a bit dull, a bit bland, a bit routine. The scene between Harper and Michael Fletcher had stirred my hormones. The rock session had got my adrenaline flowing. I was hot to trot with nowhere to go. Except my room. Where I could be alone. Lie on my bed. Play with my prick and dream. A quiet hour would do me good. Then Peter would arrive. We'd go to bed, separate beds, alas, and we'd chat late into the night. I speculated on what he wore to bed. Nothing, I hoped. The central heating was burning up the building. Windows were flung open to the September night. Boxer shorts. A cute little slip. I'd settle for whatever I could get. I'd lie on my bed and flick through the possibilities. Life wasn't too bad after all. No. Be fair. Life was fucking Ace! and about to get Acier!

I stepped into my room and noticed a bed lamp was on. Alan's angle-poise. He must have left for the wedding in a hurry. No, he was still there, lying on his bed. Had he shrunk? He was certainly smaller than I remembered him from breakfast.

Of course it wasn't Alan. I crossed the room and stood between our beds, feeling like Baby Bear in Goldilocks. "Who's this sleeping on my bed?"

Michael Fletcher! What was a First Year squirt doing lying on my bed—sound asleep? I sat at the edge of the bed and examined the intruder. He was lying on his back, face to the wall, thumb in his mouth, knees spread akimbo. Fletcher was wearing white tennis shorts with a red stripe round the waist band, a short-sleeved light-blue Aertex shirt, white socks. He'd been gracious enough to place his trainers neatly at the bottom of the bed. No harm done, but what on earth was he doing here?

I've never met a boy yet who likes to be called pretty, but Michael Fletcher was close to it. Delicate face, delicate eyebrows, thick eyelashes, a lower lip that almost pouted. Snub nose splashed with freckles. Fine, straight hair, fringed at the front, floppy on his neck. Delicate features, but a strong little body that filled out his T-shirt and tennis shorts. Strong legs, dimpled around his knees, the right one carrying two or three traditional scabs.

There was the hint of blue beneath his eyes. This was a tired boy. But this was no place for him to sleep his tiredness away. With my fingertips I pushed the hair back from his forehead. I let them run down his cheek, across his mouth. I felt a whisper of breath. My fingers continued across his neck, across his chest and down to his stomach. His T-shirt had rolled up from his waist, revealing a creamy expanse of flesh still kissed by the summer sun. A few tickles should wake sleeping beauty up. I ran my finger tip round and round his belly button, an inner for the record. The boy gave a squeak, moved his head slightly, sucked on his finger, then subsided into stillness. There are terrible temptations that require strength, strength and courage, strength and an incipient erection to give in to. I got that or something like it from *An Ideal Husband*, too.

My finger ran circles in his tummy button. I traced a delicate blue vein that ran down his left inner hip and disappeared below the waistband of his tennis shorts. My finger traced his baby's bottom skin along the edge of his waistband, slipping into the hollows on either side. Guilt pricked my back if not my thumbs as I thought of the wicked things I wanted to do. For a moment I tried to analyse why I wanted to do them. I shrugged my shoulders. What the hell?

I bent over the sleeping boy's tummy and ran the wet tip of my tongue along the creamy skin above his waistband. Back and forth went my tongue, slipping at the end of each trip into the hollow of his hip. What would it take to wake this sleeping beauty up? With the thumbs of each hand, I edged up his T-shirt until his stomach and chest were bare under my lips.

I was beginning to feel silly when I noticed the hillock beneath his tennis shorts. A little mound had appeared in Michael Fletcher's crotch. Was he still asleep? My mouth slid down to the hillock. My lips exerted the lightest pressure. I could feel him growing under my lips. The boy was getting an erection! My fingers replaced my lips. My fingers searched out his penis below the thin fabric below the thin cotton and gently squeezed either side until he had a full-blown hard-on. His legs stirred. He spread them further apart. I know an invitation when I feel one.

What was I doing? I don't think it was sex, not quite yet. It was an experiment, an irresistible experiment. A boy was lying on my bed, sleeping, his thumb in his mouth, his prick as hard as a milk bottle. Little Michael Fletcher. What a day he was having! How much did he know about sex? Was this afternoon his first encounter? Was he old enough to have wet dreams? Did he toss himself off yet? Had he ever been seduced? Would he like to be seduced? Would he like me to seduce him? To initiate him? I squeezed his prick a little harder.

Michael's eyes flickered open. His eyes were sleepy, glazed. He blinked some of the sleep away. He looked less sleepy, more bewildered. I watched him coming to himself. He raised his head from my pillow. I pushed him back down.

"It's okay, Fletcher. I mean Michael. (Oh, what the fuck.) Mike." His eyes were huge. "I'd like an explanation. Why are you sleeping on my bed? Take your time. I'm not angry."

The squirt slid a hand into the right hand pocket of his shorts and pulled something out. It glittered in the light. "It's this. I found this. I think it's yours." He stretched out his hand. On the palm lay my plectrum. I took it from his hand and held it to the light. Yes, it was mine. I gave a low whistle of relief. The plectrum meant a lot to me.

"Thanks, Mike. Where'd you find it? In the music room?" The boy nodded and risked a smile. "I was looking for you. I couldn't find you. Then I tried your room. I thought I'd wait for you a bit." He blushed. "I lay down on your bed. I was remembering this afternoon. I must have fallen asleep. You don't mind, do you? I didn't mean any harm. I sort of…missed you." Was this squirt simple? You didn't make declarations like that to other boys, especially not older boys in an all-boys' school. And especially not, if you were as close to being pretty as this boy was. I leaned over him.

His head lay on the pillow, my hands on either side. He smiled up at me as I smiled down at him. I blushed as I remembered how my fingertips and lips had brushed his body. I glanced down to see if his hard-on had subsided.

The clasp of his shorts were open. The zip pulled down. One flap open to the right. Mike wore a white slip with blue dolphins. His erection was clearly outlined as it pushed the fabric upwards. One hand cupped his balls. I looked back at his face. Blank. expressionless. I sat back from his body. I reached down and grasped his T-shirt. He half-sat as I slid it over his head. He lay back down, hands clasped under his head.

As if I'd been given lessons, I tilted his head back and kissed his throat. I let my lips slide onto his chest, skin smoother than my own. I gave his nipples tiny kisses, then slid my lips over them and sucked wetly, my thumbs sliding into the curves of his hairless armpits. My lips slid from his chest, across his stomach. My tongue probed the elastic frontier of his cotton briefs. Mike's hand came to push them down; my fingers urged him away. Wet lips on warm dolphins.

My tongue traced the hardness of his erection, my lips slid to either side of his shaft, squeezing as my fingers had. Squeezing, sucking, for five, six, seven minutes. I drew my head back. The boy's penis was outlined in wet, pink, hot, hard flesh. I slipped my fingers into the waistband of his briefs. It was time. He raised his bottom from the bed. I eased them down, across his hips, across his groin, down his legs to his knees.

His prick sprang free, taut, tight, hard, painfully erect, burstingly erect against my lips. I could feel the boy throb and pulsate against my cheek, my nose, my lips, as I ran him across my face. Then I swallowed him whole, his prick, his balls, into the hot, wet cavern of my urgent mouth. I squeezed and sucked, let his ballsac roll on my tongue as his prick found its way to the roof of my mouth, into the hot, wet, grasping dark of my throat. I paused and held him there. I could feel his heart beating in the throbbing of his shaft. I could feel his hands in my hair, grasping, gripping, holding tight. I released his balls to have more leverage on his prick. My head began to bob over his smooth, sweet crotch. His penis slid in and out of my mouth, in to the hilt, out to the tip, then in again. Michael's hips were moving now, his bottom rising and falling from the bed. Voluntary? Involuntary? It didn't matter. We were both out of control. That was all that mattered.

When the boy came, it was quick and sudden. His body shook and trembled all over. I could feel him shudder as if he was having a minor fit. My hands held his hips, fingers massaging the flesh deep on either side as if I were pumping the sperm out of him.

"Oh! Oh! Oh!" The voice was high and light, the sounds strangled, filled with delight and shame at his delight. The sounds fragmented as he squirted himself into me. Hot little jets of fluid hit the back of my throat, his prick pulsating, throbbing, jumping with every release. For a moment I was frightened for him. The boy was cumming, cumming hard, maybe for the first time, maybe unexpectedly. I remembered my first time. I'd thought I was dying. And I'd wanted to die again and again.

Two or three minutes ticked by. I let the boy's penis slid from my lips leaving behind its salty sweetness. One hand shielded his eyes, the other traced his balls which had risen high in their sockets. His lips moved. "Gosh, Tilson, that was amazing. I thought I was dying."

Gently I moved his hand away from his eyes and smiled to reassure him he was alive. A sheen of perspiration covered his face, the shadow on his lip declaring the manhood to become. His hair was damp and clung to his forehead. His eyelashes, sticky with sweat, fringed those huge eyes.

I was puzzled. "Mike," I asked, "when I 'saved' you from Harper, you sounded like you didn't even know that sex existed. And what was all that stuff about being initiated?"

Fletcher laughed, his voice like the chimes we had at home at Christmas.

"Oh, I made all that up. I thought Harper might leave me alone if he thought I was a kid, a baby, you know. Then you came along, my knight in shining shorts, and saved me."

I had underestimated this boy.

"And were you really asleep when I came in this evening?" I asked.

Michael Fletcher looked up at me and grinned. "That's for me to know, and you to guess." He snuggled into me. "Is it my turn to do you? Will I be 'initiated' then?" I laughed and brushed the hair from his eyes.

"We'll see," I said. "How do you feel?"

"Fine," Michael yawned. "But I'm a bit sleepy. Could I rest

a bit? But then..." He paused shyly, "...I'd like to do you."

"Turn over on your front," I instructed him. "Have a little rest. I'll tell you about the birds and the bees, and about cocks and robbers."

The boy turned over, cradling his head on his right arm. He drew his left leg up a bit making himself comfortable. I looked down at his naked body. The thick hair. The delicate neck. The surprisingly broad shoulders. The slim torso and tiny waist. Skin so clear, so fine, so delicate it was almost translucent. My thumbs seemed huge as they pressed into the pale flesh of his buttocks. Michael wriggled and opened his legs wider. I was in a quandary. The boy was beautiful. I'd just sucked him off. It was more than likely he'd do the same for me. Did that make me a D.O.M.? A dirty old man? A chaser of little boys. A paedophile! I'd found the word in my summer reading.

Was I a fifteen year old paedophile? Could anyone be a paedophile at fifteen? Let's say I was in the park. And a paedophile approached me. And wanted to do things to me. Would I suddenly stop being a paedophile? Or could one paedophile do things to another paedophile? I shrugged my shoulders. It was too complicated for me. I was doing what I was doing because I enjoyed doing it. And presumably Michael Fletcher enjoyed what I was doing. I couldn't see where the harm was.

My thumbs had been caressing the meat of Michael's buttocks. His hands slipped down, grasped a buttock each and pulled them apart. It looked as if Mike was as interested in experimenting as I was. I edged down the bed to sit just below his bum. My thumbs helped separate his cheeks. His bum was like a tight little peach. It even had a little peach fuzz. I lowered my face into the crack. A little smelly but the smell was sexy. I watched his skin darken as it reached the centre. There was a little hole, like a small brown mouth, with a pinkish ring as its lips. Slightly serrated lips.

With my thumbs, I gently edged the lips apart. Darkness. Reddish brown flesh edging into darkness. I leaned over and blew a stream of air into the hole. Why did I do that? I hadn't the faintest idea. It just seemed the right thing to do. I blew again and again. It must have been the right thing for Michael edged his fingers down the inner walls of his cheeks so he could stretch them even wider. I suddenly felt like.... Oh, fuck it, I felt like it, so I did.

I ran the tip of my tongue around the perimeter of the boy's pooh ring. That's what we called them in the showers. "Suck my pooh ring," someone would shout in insult. Why was that insult such a delightful prospect now? If you'd asked me, even earlier that afternoon, if I'd like to suck a twelve-year-old boy's pooh ring, I would have been mortified with embarrassment and anger. All that had gone. Licking, sucking, kissing Michael Fletcher's anal ring, his sphincter, seemed the most natural thing in the world. I prised the little lips apart and stuck the tip of my tongue in as far as I could go.

"Upstairs" there was another grunt of pleasure. Michael twisted his body to make his erection more comfortable. My hand slid to my lap and opened my buttons. I had no intention of trying to bugger the boy; his asshole was so small I couldn't get much more than half my tongue in. Six inches of throbbing meat seemed out of the question. But I knew what I wanted to do. I wanted to have a wank, toss myself off, masturbate, and smear the cum into his little hole. Why? I haven't the faintest idea. It just seemed the thing to do.

Kneeling between the boy's outstretched legs, I worked my cock. It was throbbing, aching. I knew it would be only a matter of seconds before I came. I'd fire most of into his crack, smear some more across his back, and as he turned to look up at me, smear some more across his lips, and then I'd... My hand was a blur on my hot, hard prick, the cum was boiling in my ballsac, when…

A splash of light. On and off.

"Oh, sorry, I'll come back later."

And Peter was gone.

I swung myself off the bed, my erection subsiding a little. I turned Michael around. His eyes were glazed with sleep and desire. "What's up?" he asked, sounding perilously close to Bugs Bunny.

"Nothing," I said. "Nothing," pushing my hard-on with difficulty back inside my trousers. "But you've got to go. Peter Parker's staying here tonight." I helped Michael back into his shorts and shirt. It didn't take long. He sat on the edge of the bed working his laced-up gym shoes back onto his feet. "Has Parker been initiated? Are you going to do him tonight?" I laughed, but it was hysteria, not humour.

"May I see you tomorrow, Tilson?" asked Michael shyly. "I really enjoyed this evening. Are we going to do it again?"

I sat on the edge of the bed with this twelve-year-old ingenue standing between my legs. I felt like his fucking father! "I don't know, Mike. I'm awfully busy tomorrow. We'll see. But, uh, Mike…" A pause. "Don't talk about this to…" He cut me short. "Look, Tilson, I may only be First Year, but I'm not a fucking idiot. I'm not going back to the dorm to shout, 'Hey, you guys, guess what? Guy Tilson just sucked me off.' Give me a break, Guy." I pulled Mike to me, gave him a hug, kissed him on the forehead, turned him round, smacked him on the bottom and sent him on his way, laughing.

An hour later as we lay in bed, Peter in Allen's, I in my own, I popped the question. We'd had a great conversation about possible numbers for the band and had listed half a dozen for further consideration. But I couldn't go to sleep without asking. "Peter, do you want to know what was going on? I mean when you came in earlier." He turned on his pillow to face me. I appreciated that.

"No, not really. This is my first boarding school, first all boys' school. I expected it to be different to what I've been used to."

"But did I offend you?" I asked.

"Did you hurt that boy?"

"No, of course not."

"Did he want you to do things to him?"

"Yes, I believe he did."

"Did he enjoy them…the things, I mean?"

"Yes, I know he did."

"Then it's none of my business. Now, let's get some sleep. We've got a lot of playing tomorrow."

I sighed in relief. Then I asked, "Peter, how was it with Dr Moonie this evening?"

After a pause, Peter replied, "That is none of your business."

This time we both laughed.

"G'night."

"G'night."

Chapter 5

After a mixed spell at the beginning of the term, the weather sorted itself out, and during the next fortnight we were able to get in regular hockey practice every afternoon. Ackerley, the Head Boy, was captain of the 2nd XI, and he told me there was a chance I might get a permanent spot in the side, which made me keener than ever.

My opinion of Ackerley was changing rapidly. His quiet manner concealed a strength and a steadiness which surprised a lot of people. I noticed that Bully Boy Harper and his cronies regarded him warily, and on the only occasion when I saw them up to their old tricks—which, in this case, consisted of trying to make things uncomfortable in the showers for one of the smaller chaps—Ackerley called them aside. He didn't seem to say much, but the persecution stopped.

The term was four weeks old when Tony came to our Saturday evening pop rehearsal brimming with good news. Even the fact that Tim was off home for the weekend and Peter was 'having a session' with Dr Moonie couldn't shake his good mood.

"There's an inter-schools music festival in Cambridge just before the end of term. The rules say any kind of musical combination can enter. I've just talked it over with the Head and he says that, as long as the school isn't put to any major expense, and as long as it doesn't interfere with our school work, we can enter." He grinned his special grin. "We'll have to practice like fury. I don't see why we shouldn't pull it off."

"But what about getting there?" My natural caution asserted itself. "By the end of term, I'm always broke."

"Oh, that's all right," said Tony. "I'll persuade the old man to send the school minibus. Now what can we work on till your precious Peter gets here?" There was a pause. Tony laughed. "I've got it. You can work on my 'precious peter' till Parker gets here."

Tony's laughter was throaty enough for me to know he was serious. We hadn't had sex since before the summer holidays. I'd been distracted by Peter Parker and young Michael Fletcher. I'd forgotten what a startlingly handsome chap Tony Honeyman was. "God, I'm horny," he said, openly rubbing his crotch. "The idea of the festival has got me over-excited. I won't be able to concentrate until I get some kind of relief." He grinned that grin. "I hope you're not going to play hard to get with me." He reached behind him and twisted the dimmer until the lights in the room were way down low.

My eyes got accustomed to the darkness. I offered no resistance as Tony pulled me down onto a pile of rubber gym mats. I began caressing his shoulders, he started running his hands up and down on my back. We soon were undressing. My heart was beating so hard I thought it would explode. Tony had seduced me when I first came to Abertay. The old magic was still there. It was amazing the way he could switch to being so romantic. As in everything else, Tony Honeyman committed himself a hundred percent.

My hands shook as I unbuttoned his shirt. He'd pulled my shirt up out of my pants and was running his hand over my stomach. He opened up my shirt, leaned over me and ran his wet lips round my belly button. It was a simple act, but amazingly erotic. My prick sprang to full attention in seconds. It was kind of strange as we fumbled with each other's trousers at the same time; my fingers were shaking which added to the delicious tension of it all. I wondered how much Tony had grown down there during the summer.

We both had our shirts off. I slowly massaged his pectorals. They were hard, with very pointed nipples. His fingernails were lightly scratching my own little rosebuds. I was in ecstasy.

We stopped kissing. I removed Tony's pants and slowly pulled down his boxer shorts. Beautiful! The soft light glistened on his legs. His pubic hair was thick and curly. His prick jutted out from his belly. I was a little shaken. Before the summer, he'd been about six inches; now he was nearer eight. I gulped as I remembered how I'd gagged on him before. How could I possibly take all of him now?!

I started to finger his balls. He whispered he wanted to see me naked. I started to unzip myself, but his hand stopped me. He began to unzip me with tantalizing slowness. My dick was straining to get out of those pants. When the zip was all the way down, he reached his hand into my pants. It took him a few seconds to finger his way into my Y-fronts, but he finally found my dick. He caressed it for a moment, then ran his hand along its length, stopping to give it a squeeze every once in a while. I was so horny, I was embarrassed. My prick throbbed between his fingers, the head already wet and slippery, the foreskin pulled all the way back.

Tony finally released it from my underpants and pulled them down. He rubbed my penis and whispered in my ear that it was the longest he'd seen on a boy my age. That made me feel good, because I wasn't sure how I measured up against other boys. I saw plenty of naked genitals in the showers and in the dormitories, but not in full erection.

Tony was lying on top of me, his nipples rubbing on my chest as mine kissed his. We rolled around for quite a while, fondling and rubbing each other.

Unexpectedly, he knelt and put his head over my crotch. Opening his mouth, he lowered his head and guided my dick into his warm mouth. Once more I was startled. I'd sucked Tony off several times, but this was the first time he'd done it to me.

My hands surrounded his head; his soft hair was tantalising. I don't know if my hands were guiding his head as it started going up and down, or if I was more of a spectator, but he was sucking and sucking on my swollen dick as my hands rubbed the back of his neck. Up and down he went, sucking and pulling on it. I wanted to shoot, but suddenly he stopped. "It's your turn", he said. He lay back on the blanket.

I moved my head over his prick. My mouth closed in, my tongue slowly entered his cock slit. He was wet. His juices were flowing, he was sweaty and greasy. I curled my tongue and stuck it in as far as I could, flicking it against anything I could find. I sucked and gulped as I swallowed as much of his cock as I could. Tony started to wiggle around and it was hard to keep my tongue moving. Just as I was starting to really get into it, he pushed me away and said, "I want to feel you inside me. Don't ask questions, just do it."

If I'd been startled before, I was stunned now. This was quantum leap. This was the real thing. This was buggery. And I was doing the buggering! I'd always expected this is what Tony would ask of me. Now here we were, lying on the gym mats in the music room on a Saturday night, preparing for me to bugger the Headmaster's son. I remembered the school motto: 'Upwards to Glory!' Who was I to deny our collegiate destiny?

I licked my hand and run my fingers round his cock. Tony was as soppy wet, slippery and gooey as me. I spat two or three times into my hand. I rubbed the mixture of cock juices and saliva on my dick before I lay along him full length, belly to belly. I slid lower so that I could slide my cock up his crack until it touched his most tender spot. Part of me wanted to get my face into Tony's crack and observe that most beautiful of all human orifices; part of me was downright scared I'd chicken out if I saw where my penis was going—right into Honeyman's shithole.

My dick was the longest I could ever remember. "Put it in me, put it all inside me," he whispered. I guided it to the ring and slowly started pushing it in. He was really hot down there. He swung his legs up round my waist and locked his ankles behind the small of my back. The image itself was enough to stiffen my prick until it throbbed and pulsated; the head was gripped as if by an elastic band.

Tony's eyes were closed but I could see his eyes were moving beneath the lids. I pushed my dick into him as far as I could while he kept moaning, "All the way, all the way." I started to move my hips up and down, up and down. We kissed again, long kisses, our tongues sliding against each other as we sucked at each other's mouths. I felt his prick burning against my belly each time I pushed harder at his ring. His sphincter gave way and a third of my cock slid inside him. The muscle gripped me so tightly I was terrified for a moment it would snap me off. But instinct took over.

I kept lifting my pelvis and thrusting my dick into his hole as far as I could. Up and down, up and down I went. "Hey Stud, ride me!" he whimpered.

"Ride me". A thought flashed through my mind. It was my turn to grin. I carefully withdrew. "Just a sec. I've got an idea," I said. He opened his eyes and looked into my face.

"You really like horses, don't you?" I asked him.

"You know I'm crazy about them," Tony said. "They mean as much to me as music and…sex," he said with a twinkle in his eye. I looked into his face for a minute or two and then stood up. He started working his hard-on. "Where are you going?" he asked.

"I'll be right back," I told him, stepping out of my trousers and underwear. It felt a little strange to walk across the Music Room, semi-naked, my stiff penis, smelling of Tony, bouncing against my belly. I slipped into the store room. There they were. Three saddles, leather and chrome gleaming. Horse blankets neatly shelved, the other accoutrements hanging from hooks. I recognised Tony's saddle immediately. I'd seen it often enough as he rode his colt, Ponyboy, across the evening fields.

I got Ponyboy's saddle, a horse blanket and a set of reins and took them back to where Tony was lying, on his back, naked from the waist down, playing with his huge hard-on. A smile curled his mouth.

I laid the saddle next to him, draped the blanket over us and hung the reins over my shoulders. The blanket itched somewhat, but at that point, I didn't care. I fondled Tony's ass and pressed my fingertip against his hungry hole. He got my drift and lay over the saddle, his bottom high in the area. I pulled his buttocks as far apart as I could. From the tin can at my side I took out a dollop of saddle grease, smeared it along my stiff penis, and then along Tony's anal ring. His moans showed how much he celebrated this moment with me. His hands slid round to help me. As I entered him again, he started playing with the saddle, rubbing the shiny leather against his erection. I started humping him again as I lay along his back. I pushed in and out, faster and faster, my belly slapping against his back, like Tony on a snare drum.

Tony was even more excited! He was wriggling away with a passion, moaning and bucking. I could feel a tingling inside my dick. I was getting ready to cum and I could feel Tony's sphincter squeezing my cock as it slid in and out.

"Fuck me with your horse dick. Touch me with your nuts," he grunted. His hands were now on my arse, his nails scratching my bottom as he urged me deeper and deeper, faster and faster! I could feel goose bumps all over my body. His body was starting to shake. He was moving with me, we were becoming one person, moving to the sounds of love-making. I was ready to cum. "I'm cumming, I'm cumming," I gasped into his ear.

"Give it to me. Cum inside me! I want to feel it!"

I came in great waves. I could feel myself squirt inside him in big shots. His mouth twisted to find mine again. We kissed and licked for quite a while, moving our bodies in time with each other. My heart was pounding, or was it his? I lay there draped over him, a fifteen-year-old boy joined to that of a sixteen-year-old by his pulsing, throbbing, shooting cock. My hand reached under Tony and I held onto him as his sperm shot out in thick, liquidy ropes that splattered onto the saddle beneath us.

We lay there for ten minutes, glazed, dazed, shattered. I slid my sloppy cock from his asshole. There was a squishy pop, and I was free. Tony rolled over onto his back and lay grinning up at me. I lay down beside him and looked up at the ceiling.

Chapter 6

"Tony, can I ask you something?"

"You can ask," he said. "That doesn't mean I'll give you answer, but you can ask." His voice was low and husky.

"Well, you know when I came to this school. When I met you. Down at the lake, I mean. Looking at the ducks." I couldn't help it. I giggled.

"Mmmmm?" Tony sounded lazily content.

"That was my first time," I said.

"I know," he said.

"When was yours? Your first time, I mean."

Tony yawned and made himself more comfortable.

"Why do you want to know?" he asked.

"I don't know," I said. "Interested, that's all. You don't have to, tell me, I mean."

A pause.

"Yeh, I'll tell you. In fact, I want to tell you. It'll bring him back, and I miss him, sometimes, even now, I miss him. I miss Eric."

"Go on."

"We haven't always had this school. We only bought it three years ago. In fact, I went to a state school. My father was in Germany, making money, and connections. We didn't want to spend money on fees, not even on a minor school like Abertay. So, I went to a state school. In Scotland of all places. My mother is Scottish. Did you know that?"

"No, I didn't."

"I was twelve, going on thirteen. I'd just started at a Scottish boys' school, an academy, as they called it. It was mid-September. You often have an Indian summer in Scotland in September and October. It was warm, balmy and sunny. At lunchtimes, a lot of boys used to go down onto the lower playing fields for a game of football. I must have been a bit weird even then because I actually wanted to play in goal—no self-respecting Scottish schoolboy ever does! But I was English, a Sassenach, so I was expected to be a bit weird.

"The lower playing fields were at the bottom of this huge crater in the ground which had been grassed over by the years. That day was really warm. Everyone had his blazer and tie off (strictly forbidden, but few teachers came near the 'crater'). We had a really good game. Everyone was hot and sticky. The first bell went and most people grabbed their stuff and headed up the hill. A few of us die-hards went on playing. Then the second bell went. Seconds later, there was only Eric and myself left, with Eric taking a few last pot shots at me in goal.

"I didn't know Eric well. Eric had money. I had brains. But Eric was fun, and I appreciated how much he'd befriended this 'fish out of water'. Even though we'd been at the school for less than a month, Eric was a popular boy. Not bright but generous. Not intelligent but funny. Athletic. And extremely good-looking."

Tony sighed and played with his cock. I felt a pang of jealousy and played with mine.

"Good-looking. Well-built, regular features, open face, freckles, well-cared-for teeth. And a big prick. A very big prick. An outstandingly big prick! After games, we'd all pile into the communal showers. It came as a bit of a shock to me, but after a couple of sessions, I didn't give a toss, so to speak. Of course, we all sneakily checked each other out in the showers: that's what pubescent, adolescent boys do. Some boys got erections and were ribbed unmercifully, but all of it was done in good humour.

"Ten inches. That's what they said Eric had—ten inches. I remember it as being long and thick, but it wasn't ten inches. It was just under eight. I know, I measured it. Eric would stand there starkers, toweling himself down, with his hose pipe bouncing between his legs, with half the room taking sneaky peeks while the other half called out ribald comments. Eric ignored the lot of them.

"The only boy amongst First Year who could rival Eric was —me. Don't get me wrong. I'm not boasting. I didn't have ten or even eight inches, but I did have six inches, a thick six inches. Somebody asked me how I'd managed to get such a big dick. I told them the truth: I hadn't the faintest idea. But I had something else many of the other boys didn't have: pubic hair, lots of it, thick, curly, dark brown pubic hair. Eric was reddish blond, so what he had didn't show up so much. It felt good to be one up on him, at least in one area.

"Back to that September day. We grabbed our blazers, ties and shirts (yes, Eric and I'd gone that far in breaking the rules) and started to scramble up the grassy hill. Eric was behind me. He slipped (he said), grabbed for something, got me, and together we tumbled back down the hill. We ended up in a heap of arms, legs and clothing. Then it happened."

Tony was erect again, so was I.

"Eric shifted till he was sitting astride me. He put his knees on my arm muscles, such as they were, pinning me to the grass. He was looking down into my face. He reached behind him and stroked my genitals! I was stunned. My face, already red from the football, burst into flames. I tried to heave him away, but he bore down on me, not enough to hurt, just enough to pin me there, and kept stroking me, his fingers fumbling till he found my cock.

"I'm not sure what I would have done if Eric hadn't kept looking straight into my eyes. His hair flopped over his face. He was sweating. He pushed the hair out of his eyes and kept looking at me. I turned my head away, turned it back, closed my eyes, opened them.

"Fuckin' hell! I was getting an erection! I had an erection. I grew stiff and hard under his touch. His fingers and thumb closed round my hard-on and began working the skin along the shaft. 'Do I have to hold you down?' he asked. I shook my head from side to side. Eric slid from my body and we lay side to side. He was still manipulating me. 'We can't stay here,' he said. 'I know,' I said. 'The sheds,' he said. I nodded.

"We scrambled up, grabbed our clothes and headed across the fields, away from the school.

"The 'sheds' was the polite name for the boys' latrines on the far side of the playing fields. Smoking went on there. Everybody knew that. So did sex, but I was too slow to know that. Eric wasn't.

"We got to the sheds and slipped inside. I was trembling, so was Eric. He took our blazers and ties and hung them on a hook on the back of the shed door. 'I'll go first,' he said. I nodded, not sure what he intended.

"Eric sat down on one of the toilets and pulled me towards him. He opened my belt, unbuttoned my flies, then dragged down my flannels and Y-fronts to my ankles. I was exquisitely embarrassed. My cock was hard and already slick with pre-cum. Eric fondled me for a bit, then without a by-your-leave opened his mouth and sucked me in as far as my prick would go. I almost fainted! The idea of sucking someone's prick had never crossed my mind even in my wilder masturbatory fantasies."

I began stroking my own stiff member more rapidly as I listened.

"I stood there and watched my penis slide in and out of Eric's mouth, fascinated by the way it bulged his cheeks, amazed that he could get so much of me inside him. It felt so good! Where was it all going—down his throat? I put my hands on his head and instinctively, I suppose, began pushing and pulling to find the rhythms I liked best. One of Eric's hands worked the base of my cock while the other played with my balls. Wonderful! But when his lower hand slipped into my crack and headed for my bumhole, that was too much! I clenched my hole and clasped my legs together. Eric didn't persist.

"He brought me to the brink of orgasm at least five times. My prick was going frantic, my heart was racing. When I thought I couldn't stand any more, he let me cum—he let me cum in his mouth! I couldn't believe it. We'd done a bit of biology in junior school, so I knew what semen was (and I'd done my own 'research' in the school library), but for someone to actually swallow it! Eric's gulps filled the stinking shed. At that moment it was the most romantic place on the planet.

"He waited until I'd relaxed completely, slipped me out, took a handkerchief from his pocket and wiped my cock and his lips. Sheer class!

"It was my turn. To be honest I panicked a bit. 'You don't have to use your mouth if you don't want to,' said Eric reassuringly. 'Your hand will do fine.' I took this as a personal challenge and swallowed every drop he shot down the back of my throat." I shuddered deliciously at the thought. But he continued.

"Ten inches? No. But it was challenge enough to get even four inches of Eric's cock into my mouth. 'What do we do now?' I squeaked as we did up our buttons, pulled on blazers, knotted each other's ties, and considered our strategy for the rest of the afternoon.

"'We can't get back into school,' said Eric. 'They'll have done the register by now. Let's think. Yes, you got too much sun at lunchtime. You threw up. I was worried, so I took you home. I live in the Perth Road. We'll go there. Look sick. I can talk my mother into anything. We'll get a note from her. Then we'll come back to school; that'll look good. No. On second thoughts, we won't come back to school this afternoon. My mother will tell you—us—to stay at home for the rest for the afternoon. Then at half three we'll go swimming. How does that sound?'

"'Brilliant,' I said.

"'Let's go,' he said.

"Eric and I had sex together for the whole year. It was all wonderfully uncomplicated. We were faithful to each other. We were in the same cricket, football and tennis teams. We discovered anal sex together. I was in every top academic set, Eric in every bottom set.

"At the end of the year, school year, we came back south. My father bought into Abertay and…you know the rest."

"Do you keep in touch with Eric?"

"No," said Tony. "We wrote a couple of letters, then postcards, but then… We had a great time, great sex, great fun, then it was over. That's the way it should be," he added, "at least when you're kids. And that's what we are. Kids. So let's not get too serious. What's the time? Do you want to suck this for me? Have we got time?"

I glanced at my watch.

"Shit! Look at the time. Peter could walk in any second. He's already late. Come on," I panicked.

"Oh my God," mimicking Mortimer, "we can't let Peter see us like this. The shock might be too much for him—and you!" Tony was taking the piss, but not too unkindly. Athletically, he flipped to his feet in a handspring of sorts, pulled up his shorts and trousers and zipped himself. "Well, boy, I'm ready to play. Music, I mean. What about you?" I pulled myself together, feeling just as sticky and gooey as Tony must have felt. "Thanks, Tony," I mumbled. "I'll do the same for you some time."

"I should bloody well hope so," he laughed, feeling his arsehole through his trousers. "Shit, I'm sore back here. Bet I'm red raw. You've certainly grown in the summer." I blushed in delight. "Mind you, you're still a virgin, and we can't have that in The Ram Stams. Let that wait. We've got music to play." As he spoke, he bent and wiped the cum that had splattered across the saddle. He was just in time. As he finished, Peter Parker came panting through the main door.

Chapter 7

"Sorry, I'm late," he gasped. "I've run all the way. It isn't easy to get away from Dr Moonie on a Saturday night. I hope you guys started without me." Tony and I exchanged grins. Peter gave us his puzzled look. He almost sniffed the air. The smell of sex was all around us. Tony broke the tension. "Great news, Parker. We've got ourselves a music festival. Tilson, get the amps set up while I do my drums. We've gotta lotta music to make tonight."

We got underway. Tony introduced us to a song he was writing with the festival in mind. The song was certainly funny although I thought some of the verses might not go down too well if there were any strait-laced masters amongst the judges. We gave the number, called 'Ride, Pony, Ride' a good run through. Then we worked on the Stones' 'Jumpin' Jack Flash' and made quite a good fist of it. Two hours flashed by.

"Right! Time's up," called Tony. "Peter, you get to work on those lyrics. Get them into your head. Your voice is great but we'll have to work on your movement a bit. Have you ever seen Mick Jagger?" Peter shook his head dubiously. "Watch Top of the Pops. They're on tomorrow night. That'll give you an idea. Get that pelvis moving. It's just like screwing standing up." Peter blushed furiously. "Sorry," laughed Tony. "I'd forgotten you were one of Dr Moonie's boys."

We packed things away, including the saddle and riding gear. I don't know how Peter resisted asking what they were doing lying in the middle of the music room." He'd probably worked out that discretion was the better part of valour. We walked in silence back to the dorms, but it wasn't a heavy silence. We simply enjoyed each other's company.

I was still agog that I'd screwed Tony Honeyman in the arse. He was strolling across the playing fields with my sperm up his anal canal. I thought of the millions of little tadpoles carrying my genes swimming blindly up his shit tract on the road to nowhere. What must they be thinking? And soon, Tony'd be sitting in his bedroom study, probably chatting to Ackerley or some other senior while my cum and his shit trickled out of his hole. He'd take a shower. He'd be standing there, if he had any sense, with the shower head jammed up his ass, washing me away.

It was strange how little guilt I felt. Tony'd treated it all so lightly, so "matter-of-fucktly," to coin a phrase, that I couldn't get a handle on shame or guilt. We'd wanted to do it, so we did it. We'd hurt nobody. We'd enjoyed it. Did the act make us homosexual? I didn't know and I didn't much care. I fully expected I'd grow up, go to university, get a degree, a job, a car, a wife, a mortgage, a couple of kids, an overdraft, a paunch, maybe a divorce, marry again, and then keel over with cancer of the colon, or something like that, and that it would all be over. There had to be some fun along the way.

"Penny for them." That was Peter's voice. I'd forgotten he was there.

"Sorry, Peter, I was dreaming."

"Not of Michael Fletcher, I hope," laughed Peter. "He's a bit small for you. And you don't really want a First Year squirt hanging round your neck, do you?"

"No, not exactly," I laughed in reply, "though there is one place I wouldn't mind him hanging round." I'd no clear image of what that would involve, but we both laughed anyway. It was good to see Peter taking Fletcher and myself so lightly. I dearly wanted to ask Peter if he was interested in… I wasn't sure how to put it… I drew back from the thought. Ram Stam was going so well that I didn't want to introduce anything that made the boy uncomfortable. Let him get used to the idea first.

I said "Good night," Peter said "God bless," and we made our way to our separate rooms. A few minutes later I was tucked up under my duvet, my hand caressing my stiff cock as I replayed the music room movie over and over again in my mind. My cock was too raw and tender for any real work, and I fell asleep as snug as my hard prick up Tony's rectum had been.

The term went on more or less as usual. We managed to rehearse four or five times a week, and I thought our programme was getting pretty good—much better than some of the groups I heard on the school record player. The only real problem was Peter's body movements. I've seen a sexier fish finger. He'd stand there, pouring out raw sex from his throat and from his guitar, while his hips twitched spasmodically. It was more embarrassing than erotic, and the more you mentioned it, the more Peter froze. In the end, Tony told him to move as little as possible. At least that would be something different!

To my great joy I got my place in the 2nd XI and played in a match against our closest rivals—a school from Norfolk. I can't say I excelled myself, but I didn't do too badly. Ackerley was pleased with me.

"Well played," he said, clapping me on the back. "But you're limping. I saw that blond shit take you out with his stick. How could the ump. have missed it?"

I laughed. "No, I'm not limping because of that. I've broken two studs on my right boot." Ackerley looked relieved. "I'll have a helluva job getting the stumps out," I said. "I haven't got a key."

Ackerley looked at me, a little curiously, I thought. "Come over to the Sixth. There's probably no-one there. The First XI have taken an entire busload of supporters to Norwich. I've got a key. I'll have those stumps out in a jiffy. That's the least you deserve after that hammering you took."

I limped along beside Ackerley. He was right. The Sixth Form block was empty. We went straight to his room. He found the key and wrestled with the stumps. It proved a more difficult job than he'd thought. He turned on 'Sports Report' at five o'clock and we got all the football news from the First Division. Arsenal 3 Man. United 2. My joy was complete. It took Ackerley twenty minutes to wrestle the stumps free. He got up and handed me my boots. Then came that curious look again.

"You've missed hot showers," he said.

Ackerley was right. After a match, there was a stampede to the junior showers. The hot water lasted for about half an hour. Now I was faced with tepid at best, freezing at worst. Ackerley laughed, reached for a beach towel on his bed and threw it to me. "Come on. Be my guest. Treat yourself to a Sixth Form special." He opened a drawer and grabbed an identical towel, white with pale blue stripes, fluffy, warm. We made our way to the Sixth Form shower room, opulent by junior standards. No single cubicles with stained, ripped curtains, but a wide, tiled, open area with six or seven shower heads.

We stripped quickly in that unselfconscious way public schoolboys have, but I was exquisitely aware of Ackerley's body. Slim, yes, but hard and athletic. Broad shoulders tapered to a narrow waist. His buttocks were packed muscle, legs long and lean. Thick, curly red hair spread from the base of his prick up his belly, fanning out across his thighs. His nipples, too, were red, as if they'd been touched up with my mother's rouge. My cock betrayed me immediately. It began to thicken, harden, stretch out from my body with a will of its own. Acutely embarrassed, I turned to a tiled wall. I felt fingers on my shoulders. They turned me round to face Ackerley. He was smiling. "Me, too."

I looked down. His erection, hot, hard and huge, was

sticking out like a Belisha beacon. He stepped forward and the tip of his cock brushed my stomach—above my belly button! I felt my mouth water, my asshole clench. Ackerley reached out and turned on a shower. Luke warm, then hot water splashed our heads and shoulders. He leaned towards me and said, "We won't do anything if you don't want to. But I want to."

"Me, too," I croaked.

Water, hot water poured down in a steady stream over my back. Hands, his hands, running a bar of soap over my skin, slicking suds all over my body. Slippery bodies, wet and soapy, slid against each other. "I've always had a thing about showers," the Headboy whispered in my ear.

"Let me do you first," I said, picking up a bar of Wright's Coal Tar and running it over his chest, then I changed my mind. "No. Turn around. Your back first." He turned, and I began by soaping his shoulders.

I lathered his long, pale back, each of his arms, his hands, his long. bony fingers. I soaped his sides and his hips. One soapy hand kneaded his ass, first the muscled flesh of his buttocks, then between them. My hand slipped into the hot, sweaty darkness. I wished it were my face, my lips, my tongue. Would it disgust him? Or would it be another token of my desire for him, all of him?

"Stick a finger in me," he requested as if casually asking a junior to make him tea and toast. I complied with the request. My middle finger slipped easily inside him. With one hand I ran soapy circles around his chest; with the other I finger-fucked him gently, rhythmically, wondering if he was as hot and sticky as Tony up there.

"Okay." I finished the right leg, proceeded to the left, then finally arrived at the area we'd been waiting for. I slid out my finger and sniffed it. I soaped his cock between my hands, the soap slithery in my palms around his hard shaft. I dropped the bar of soap and slid my hands around in all that lovely slipperiness. I spread the lather all through his hair, all over his balls, between the cheeks of his ass.

I dropped to my knees and turned him to face me. I pressed my face against his crotch, which, being freshly washed, didn't smell much of anything. I pressed his hard cock against my cheek, skin against skin, flesh against flesh.

I took his cock into my mouth; it tasted like soapy water. The water splashed down over me. I felt his hands on my shoulders. I closed my eyes and began to suck the thick, purple head that throbbed in time with his heart. I could taste the juice oozing from his urethra.

"I love to have my mouth full of this," I said, pausing for a moment to relieve the gagging in my throat.

"I know you do," Ackerley said, running his hands through my hair. He thrust his cock against my cheek. I grabbed hold of it lovingly and rubbed across my face. I moaned. So did he as I pulled back and slid my lips over him again. I sucked until I could feel his prick throb and pulsate between my lips.

He slid my face from his cock. "Not yet. I don't want to cum yet. It's my turn to wash you." He washed my rump, one hand soaping, the other exploring my tight ass. He put his middle finger in me while he washed my pubic hair. I moaned and bent over a little, trying to give him better access.

I moaned as two fingers slid into me. I bent over further, holding on to the hot and cold taps for support, water running into my eyes. When I opened my mouth in an appreciative groan, it filled with water, but I didn't care. "It's good, so good," I moaned, like a girl in a porn video, the shower beating on my back, his huge, hard cock pressing into my crack. My legs were getting too wobbly to stand on, so he held my hips. I leaned back into him as he thrust two fingers in and out of me ruthlessly but lovingly (if such a contrast is possible).

Above the water, I heard his voice. "Can I try and put it inside you? I'll stop if it hurts." I pressed my bottom against his hot, hard prick.

Our words deteriorated into wild noises. The world was nothing more than water pouring down and Ackerley's cock trying to fill me up. I felt the tip press against my pooh ring. Again and again he pushed the head against my sphincter. For a moment my ring gave way and accepted him, but it was too much, way too much. It burned as if someone was scraping my ring with dry sandpaper. I think I screamed. Sweat was pouring down me like the water. I tried, I really tried, but in the end I had to push him away. I stood up and leaned against the tiled wall, a miserable failure.

I felt Ackerley's arms around me. He was kissing the nape of my neck. "You're right, Guy, you're right. I don't want to hurt you. It's not worth it. Having you here, like this, is enough." I felt relief surge through me. I turned to face him. He wrapped me in his arms, my head under his chin. I felt his hot cock brush mine.

We towelled ourselves dry, then went into Ackerley's study bedroom to complete what we'd started. As I turned around, he took me by the shoulders to kiss me, and, laughing, I threw my arms around his waist and pulled him onto the bed on top of me. He yelped as he lost his balance and sprawled across me in a tangle of arms and legs.

"Hey! Would you mi—" he began.

I shut him up with a kiss. His warm weight on my body, his clean, bare skin against mine, our cocks fencing... I savoured the feeling, and enjoyed a hot, slow kiss as well. When we broke, he raised my head and looked at me. "You're something else, Guy Tilson. You really are. Something else."

My arms went around him, my feet hooked round his calves to pull him as close to me as I could. A little squirming on his part brought the hard shaft of his cock along the full length of my bumhole; the hot pressure thrilled me. I rubbed myself against him. The friction made us both twitch with pleasure.

My fingers clutched at his back as he kissed my neck under my ear. I started to squirm in earnest as his lips moved along my throat. They slid over my collarbone, brushed at my chest and finally settled on my left nipple. He lipped it gently, puckered around it and sucked.

"Your tongue…your tongue…please," I gasped as his weight pushed me deeper into the mattress.

"Oh!" I cried as he flicked the tip of his tongue over my taut nipples. My back arched as he, keeping his mouth on my flesh, took his cock in hand and rubbed the head along my anal ring. I felt how slippery I'd become and thought how his full, thick length might slide into me now. He took my left nipple between his teeth and rolled it roughly, still rubbing his cock-head against me.

"Give it to me, Ackerley!" I cried, suddenly, out of control, needing to feel him inside me. He raised his head and smiled at me knowingly, then teased me some more by rubbing the tip of his dick against the entrance to my rectum.

"Please…in me…put it…in me…ahh…aaahhh!"

I opened my mouth, moaning low and throaty as I finally felt his hard cock push my sphincter aside and bore into my body.

"Ugghhhh!" I threw my hips up against him and held onto his back for dear life while he pumped violently. My legs were up over his shoulders, round his ears. When did they get up there? The wind was knocked from my lungs and I loved it, every minute. I wanted more, more, more! It was too much to keep up for long, and he slowed, then stopped, and we kissed again. I lay with my legs wrapped around him, not wanting to lose the closeness and the throbbing fullness inside me. He began again, harder, faster, deeper, into the hilt, out to the tip and in to the hilt again.

"Oh!" A gasp sprang from my lips as orgasm crept up on me and abruptly hit me full force. To accentuate my throes, he pulled almost all the way out of me and thrust back in forcefully. My fingers dug into his back and my legs flopped around his shoulders, but it felt too good to be self-conscious. As I felt him shoot his load into me, his cock expanding, throbbing, pulsating, the cum streaming up his cock canal, my own orgasm took hold. As he pulled out, I shot wads of cum into the space between our bodies. He pushed into me again, cum squelched between us.

"Shit..." I sighed, finally relaxing and lying still, breathing heavily. He brushed wisps of damp hair off my forehead and gave me that quizzical look again.

"Zat good?" he asked playfully.

"Uhhnn!" I responded

"Good?"

"Uhnn!"

"Good, huh?"

His eyes sparkled and the flush on his face deepened as he pulled out of me. The emptiness I felt was disturbing. I loved the sight, the weight, the feel, the smell of this boy-man. His smell was mingled with the not so subtle scent of my asshole. I felt faint with delight.

Chapter 8

Later we had tea and buttered scones.

"Why me?" I asked Ackerley.

"Because you're... What word can I use? ...beautiful, handsome, gorgeous, really good-looking... None of them, all of them. Because you're a boy and not a girl." (Later I understood the courage it took for Ackerley to make that confession.) Because I can trust you. You're not a fool. You're not about to run around the school blabbing you've made love to the Headboy." (I blushed at the phrase 'made love'.) Because you're sensible and sweet. No, not sweet like a girl, just sweet like yourself."

"Stop it!" I protested. "You make me sound like an angel, and all I want is a bit of sex." Ackerley looked a bit crestfallen. "No, I didn't mean it that way. I liked what we did. I'd like to do it again. But I'm not going to moon around you. I'm not going to imagine this is once-in-a-lifetime true love. I wouldn't do it with you if I didn't like you. And I wouldn't do it if I didn't trust you. You're right, Ackerley. Trust is what matters. May I have another scone?"

After that, we easily got away from the sex stuff. We talked about the hockey and the season to come; we talked about The Ram Stam Boys and the music festival; we talked about Cambridge and why Ackerley had chosen Oxford; we talked about the total eclipse due in November; we talked about Arsenal and why they were so boring; we talked about.... oh, everything under the sun and then some more. The two hours sped by too quickly and it was time to go. Outside in the dark we could hear the coach turn up the drive.

Ackerley stood up from the bed, ran his fingers across my crotch and kissed me lightly on the forehead. I stood up, grabbed his balls, not too tightly, and kissed him full on the lips. As I turned to go, he smacked me across the rump and called, "Hey, monkey dick." I turned. "Yeh, gorilla gonads." "The name's Adrian to you. Not in public. But in your stinking pit at night, call me Adrian."

"Thanks, Adrian," I chimed back, "and it's Guy to you. When you're in your pit holding that big dick of yours, just think of Guy and what you've just done to his innocent bumhole. My turn next!"

"Yummy, yummy, Guy."

"Yummy, yummy, Adrian," and I, the one-time virgin, was gone.

Half-term weekend rolled in. As most of the boys came from families who were not too well off, not many of us went away, but we had a long weekend at Miller's Farm. This was not a farm at all, but a leisure centre, also owned by Tony's father, free to us that weekend. The weather was glorious, the last burst of an Indian summer before the cruellest months set in.

On the Saturday morning about twenty of us decided to organise a cross-country chase. Tony Honeyman and Tim were picked as hares and gave us fifteen minutes start. The rest of us were hounds. They made a good use of their head start. When we started to trail them we found three ways in which we might go, and there were even branches leading from each of these. They had not been too generous with their clues, either, so before we'd gone far, we broke up into several small groups, each following a different trail.

I was trotting happily along with two second formers and Peter Parker. I was wondering why I liked Peter so much. He was not lacking in pluck; he threw himself fearlessly into any game, however fierce, and was rapidly becoming one of the best rock-climbers in the school. He had allied himself with Adrian Ackerley and several other religiously-minded boys who formed the Ethics Club run by Dr Moonie. He asked me once if I'd come to one of their discussions, but I'd been up to my navel in homework and had declined the invitation. I knew that several of the younger boys attended the club; they looked up to Peter and respected him. Even young Fletcher spoke well of him, which gave me a twinge of jealousy. I'd shrugged that off as silliness on my part.

To be honest, I really liked Michael Fletcher but I was a bit queasy about getting too involved with him. After all, he was only a First Year, and though I'd enjoyed our session together, I wanted it to end there. It was too difficult and too dangerous to be involved with a younger boy in an institution where there were so many observant eyes. At the same time, I wasn't much interested in little boys. They were an addiction I wanted to steer clear of, and they didn't have the equipment I liked!

If I'd been paying attention, I wouldn't have tripped. Suddenly I felt myself hurtling earthwards. I tried to break my fall but found my left foot trapped. I hit the ground, winded. Peter helped me into a sitting position, then worked my ankle free from the tree root that held it.

Ouch! No real damage done, but I'd definitely twisted it. Peter and the others helped me to my feet. They offered to help me back to the centre.

I experimented a little with my ankle. No great problem. "Look, chaps, I'm going to make my own way back. It's only five minutes across the fields. You get on with the run. I'll see you when you get back. Honestly, I am fine." I waved them off and hobbled towards the centre which lay like a child's Lego house across the fields.

As I hobbled through the warm stubble, my ankle eased. Before I reached the centre, I knew what I was going to do. The Jacuzzi! I'd be first to use the Jacuzzi in the swimming complex. It would be locked but we all knew where the key was. I'd slip in, have a warm soak, and be out before anyone knew I was back.

The entrance was closed, but the key was gone. I gave the door a push, it opened. I slipped quietly in. If there were any members of staff there, I wanted to see them before they saw me. If there were other intruders there, I wanted to know who they were before deciding whether to announce my presence or not.

Intruders there were.

Announce my presence I did not.

The swimming pool area was empty. The Jacuzzi was in a separate room on the other side of the pool. I slipped my running shoes off and padded in that direction. I heard them giggling before I saw them.

There was a portal in the door at my eye height. I squinted through the light mist rising from the bubbling circular pool in the centre of the room. It took a few moments to focus. At first, I pulled back and rubbed my eyes, not quite believing what I was looking at: two young naked boys playing by the Jacuzzi.

Michael Fletcher!

The other boy was a First Year squirt, too. Small, slim, dark-skinned though not coloured. Straight brown hair that was almost black. Finely-chiseled features, highlighted by deep brown eyes. A respectable cock that swung between his smooth thighs. No signs of pubic hair, his front as smooth as his bottom. His name came to me: Anthony...Jamie Anthony. I'd heard Michael mention him a couple of times but I hadn't twigged theirs was a proper friendship, a special friendship.

The boys slid in and out of the water, trying to swim in tiny circles, pushing each other under, coming up spouting bubbles like sleek dolphins. I'm not sure if dolphins spout water, but if they do, this is what they would look like.

Jamie finally came out of the water and stretched himself

out by the side of the Jacuzzi. He presented a great view to spying eyes. His semi-hard dick was uncircumcised and measured about three inches, the head tucked inside a fleshy foreskin, balls pulled up tightly to his body. To my pleasant surprise, after a few moments, Jamie bent his knees slightly, placed his thumb and two fingers around his boy-cock and skinned back the foreskin, making the pink little head appear.

"Hey, Mike. Me first?"

My heart stopped for a moment.

Michael grinned as he looked out of the pool to see Jamie skinning his dick. He climbed out of the pool and sat down at Jamie's waist. He pushed Jamie's hand aside, and fitted his fingers around Jamie's hardening penis. His friend lay back to enjoy it. Mike gently and knowingly worked his fingers up and down the length of Jamie's cock, making it grow longer and harder until it reached a solid four inches. It looked enormous on the boy's slim body.

I tried to resist temptation, I really did, but then with a sigh I gave in. Without removing my eye from the window in the door, I pushed down my shorts and briefs, letting them slide around my ankles. My rock-hard cock sprang up, standing at a perfect 45-degree angle from my body. I grasped it and stroked the skin up and down the shaft. I took it very easy. I didn't want to cum—just yet.

By this time, Jamie was moaning and telling Mike to beat him hard. "C'mon, Mike, toss me off. Oh, God, yes…toss me harder…oh, shit…yes, like that, just like that." I could see Jamie's head roll from side to side, his thick dark hair spread out wetly beneath him.

Mike increased his tempo; I increased mine. Jamie's young balls let loose and whitish precum oozed from the head of his hard-on, running down over Mike's hand and onto Jamie's little ballsac and hairless nuts. Jamie moaned and squirmed beneath Mike's motions, but never once asked him to stop or ease up. Mike continued tossing that beautiful young cock until Jamie's body began to rise and fall as he pushed his hips into the warm, steamy air.

Without warning, he fountained, spurts of cum shooting from the end of his cock, making little arcs and splattering on his belly and chest. Michael let the convulsions happen, tossing Jamie off in rapid little jerks, then pulling his foreskin as far down the shaft as it would go. Jamie's hand came down and pushed his friend's hand away. He let his head roll to the side as his little chest heaved and his bottom twitched on the wet tiles. Michael waited a minute or two, then milked the last few drops of cum from the shattered boy.

Laughing, Mike asked, "How was that?" Jamie didn't answer. He inhaled deeply several times and stretched his legs out along the tiles. Mike slid back into the pool, giving his friend a few minutes to recuperate. I slowed up the work on my cock. I knew that Jamie's orgasm wouldn't end things.

I didn't have to wait long. Jamie slipped across the tiles on his back and let himself slide into the water headfirst. I wondered why until I realised this way would leave no streaks of cum on the tiles. Good thinking, Jamie.

Jamie's head disappeared below the bubbling surface. I could almost feel his hands roaming between Mike's naked legs, playing with him, squeezing his nuts. I wished I could slip into the water, too, but that would only complicate matters. I was happy enough to play the voyeur for the moment.

Jamie's head popped out of the water as he surfaced for air. "You like?" he questioned as both of his hands surrounded and massaged Mike's genitals beneath the bubbles.

"Ummmm," was about all Mike could manage. His eyes were closed, his head slung back, his arms round Jamie's neck. I was in full erection again. Even though I could not see what was going on under the water, the moans, groans and sighs from Michael were turning me on incredibly. I could almost feel Jamie's hand stroking my own six-incher. I could hardly bear it when Jamie's head ducked under the water. The top of his head bobbed up amongst the bubbles again and again. Both hands were under the water, too. His mouth must be round Mike's cock as he held the shaft, his other hand might be between Mike's legs, a finger or two digging deeply into the boy's bum hole. It was comic when Jamie's head bobbed above the water. He spat out a mouthful, took a huge breath and ducked under again. His head appeared and disappeared at increasing speed. Another huge breath and under he want again. Michael gripped Jamie's shoulders like a drowning man.

Suddenly Mike thrashed about as his body quivered and his throbbing cock apparently released spurt after spurt of hot sperm into Jamie's busy mouth. His hands disappeared under water as he held his friend's head, lips, throat and mouth in place. A shiver of worry ran through me. What if Jamie drowned! What if he drowned while sucking Michael Fletcher off? What if they pumped his stomach for water and came up with globs of sperm! Jamie's head and shoulders appeared above water. Choking, spluttering, laughing, spitting out water mixed with the essence of Michael Fletcher. He ducked his head under and came up spouting more water. He spat a mouthful directly in Mike's face. The boys collapsed into each other's arms in a fit of giggles.

I felt myself coming. I stepped out of my trunks and ran for the pool still jerking at my cock. I think I came as I was in mid-air. I was probably squirting hot cum as my body hit the shiny, still, blue water. It was the most stunning orgasm I'd ever had. I was still cumming as I touched the bottom of the pool, my penis jerking uncontrollably.

I surfaced spouting water, shaking my head like a dog new in from the rain. When my eyes cleared, I saw them—Michael and Jamie standing naked on the edge of the pool. Michael was holding my things.

"What are you doing, Tilson?" he shouted.

"Skinny dipping!" I shouted back.

"Can we come in, too?"

"Of course, you can. Come on in. The water's great."

There was a splash on either side of me as two naked bodies hit the water. They surfaced together and gazed at me with the eyes of playful seals. The three of us burst into laughter together.

"You're breaking the rules, Fletcher," I told Michael as we trod water together.

"That's what they're for," he shot back.

"Race to the shallow end!" That was from Jamie Anthony.

"Last there sucks the other two off!" That was Jamie Anthony.

"Get ready to suck my big one!" That was me. As I cut through the water, my ankle didn't hurt at all.

I won but I didn't exact payment right then; my libido had been left floating behind me somewhere in the pool. Jamie, Michael and I spent half an hour in the pool, horsing and frolicking around. Great fun, but there'd be trouble if we were caught. We gave ourselves plenty of time to get back to the bedrooms in the Old Barn before the hares and hounds came charging across the fields to claim hot showers and a swim in that order.

Chapter 9

We were bussed to the nearest town after lunch (nobody ate anything) and I spent the afternoon with Peter. First McDonalds, then a couple of bottles of strong cider from a friendly off-licence, an hour in the park, and then onto Knowles Arcade where most of the company met up. The slot machines and electronic games were given a real hammering. I noticed young Fletcher and Anthony being fed coins by a well-dressed middle-aged man who was obviously 'taking an interest' in them. The boys pumped the money into the machines with the kind of enthusiasm that their benefactor would like to pump them. I kept an eye on them but the chap did little more than feel their collars, run his fingers across the nape of their necks and press himself discreetly against their bottoms now and again.

Time to go. I whistled to the boys. They shook hands with the fellow, strolled towards me, turned and waved him a cheery good bye. "Fucking pervert," was Michael's under-the-breath farewell, which was unsporting to say the least.

That evening there was a disco. It's hard to believe that the teachers with us would organise a disco for an all boys' school trip, but that's what they did. And we boys loved it! Of course, it was double special for Ram Stam who were the featured and only band of the evening. After an hour watching sweaty older boys paw at sweaty younger boys as they gyrated pelvically round the dance floor, Ram Stam were hot to trot. We decided to do every Rolling Stones number we knew —seven to be precise—and what with encores, reprises and jam session, we cruised non-stop for over an hour. Sweat was running rivers from the four of us as we left the stage to thunderous applause from the sweaty ranks before us. Donna Summers' *I Feel Love* poured out over the speakers. We were immediately abandoned by our adoring fans who were more interested in 'pulling' each other in the hour that remained.

I took a long refreshing piss in the bushes outside, then realised I was not alone. Beside me, pissing with equal relish was Jamie Anthony, who seemed far more interested in my equipment than his own.

"That was great," said Jamie, deadheading a few roses with accurate jets of urine. "You lot can really play."

"Thanks, Jamie," I said, forgetting to adopt the requisite supercilious pose to squirts in the First Year. "You're not so bad yourself," I added, glancing humorously at the sliver of meat between his fingers.

"Not up to your standard, though," came the riposte as he continued to check my equipment out. We tucked ourselves away and zipped up.

"You didn't collect the bet," said Jamie, cooler than the proverbial cucumber.

"What bet?" I asked, playing dumb.

"The swimming pool bet," he said. "You won, didn't you?"

"Oh that? I was only joking."

"I wasn't," came the deadpan reply. "And anyway, I saw you watching us, Michael and me, in the Jacuzzi."

I laughed out loud. "Jamie Anthony, you were in no position to see anything. Your head was under water most of the time."

It was Jamie's turn to laugh out loud. "I saw you before that. I was just showing off."

Showing off! Giving Mike Fletcher a blow job under water. That was showing off! "You're nuts, Anthony," I said. "I know," he said, adding "So what?" I admit I was intrigued. I admit I broke my promise.

"We can't stand here like this. Let's go for a walk," I said. "It's amazingly warm. Look at the stars. Not a cloud in the sky. It's more like late summer than late autumn. Let's walk up the hill and look for shooting stars."

"Come on then," said Jamie, leading the way.

We strolled off into the warm night air and talked. I found out that Jamie came from one of the better prep schools. He hadn't liked it much; the young ones acted so young, the older ones didn't want him hanging around. As we walked I let my arm brush up against him, then slid an arm round his waist.

As we walked, we talked. I let Jamie do most of the talking, while I simply asked questions. His father was a fashion designer and he'd taken Jamie on his trips and travels across Europe. He'd even let his son do some modeling on the cat walk, and Jamie was unassumingly blasé about stripping and changing amongst some of the most beautiful super-models in Europe.

"It was the guys who turned me on," laughed Jamie. In fact, his son's increasing popularity amongst some of the male models led to his father's decision to 'retire' the boy early from the fashion scene. We ended up walking clear to the other side of Miller's Farm, letting hands go as we clambered up the only hill on that part of the flat Suffolk plain.

The moon shone brightly amongst myriad stars. We sat down on a patch of long, dry grass and scanned the skies for shooting stars. I moved closer to Jamie, putting my arm around his shoulder, saying something about keeping him warm. He made no effort to pull away. After ten minutes or so of small talk I pulled him closer to me, faced towards him and kissed him lightly on the lips. I was shocked when he kissed me back, pressing his lips hard against mine, then probing at them with the tip of his tongue.

It's difficult to explain why I broke the taboo about kissing. Boys often masturbated, fellatio was common, buggery not unknown, but kissing was taboo. I can only guess I kiss so easily because we've always kissed in my family. Amongst my brothers, it's cheek to cheek, but it's still kissing. Our inheritance from my mother's side of the family, exclusively French, meant that kissing came naturally. I opened up and Jamie slid in.

I suppose, too, kissing came easily because Jamie Anthony was so beautiful. Michael Fletcher was good-looking, handsome even, but Jamie was genuinely beautiful. His eyes, skin and hair glowed with health. I could have drowned in his brown eyes. His nose was elegant; that's the only word to do it; no, Jamie, the whole boy, was elegant, exquisite. Jamie was beautiful, not just beautiful but poignantly beautiful. It made me sad to think that his beauty would never be rewarded, never find its reason, never get to the bottom of itself. I didn't mind being the one who would understand it for him. Jamie was beautiful in order to give me pleasure.

We kissed for minutes, tongues probing as we did. I let my hand slide under his shirt, coming to rest on his barely developed chest. His flesh was warm and alive. I felt his starfish nipples brush the back of my hand. I wanted to see him. Why? I don't know. I'd seen naked boys all my life, including my own brothers, and though some had aroused me, there was little of this breathless, desperate excitement I felt at seeing Jamie Anthony. Of course I'd seen him at the swimming pool, but that was not the same. At the pool, his body had belonged to him, not to me; now he was giving it to me, it was mine. I wanted more than the body, I wanted what it represented, what it masked, what is sheathed: I wanted Jamie's soul. Of course I know there's no such thing as the soul, but it symbolised something about Jamie that I wanted, needed, and, to use the ultimate taboo word amongst schoolboys, loved.

With no hesitation or resistance from him, I undid the buttons to his shirt and let it fall away to the sides of his body. His skin was smoother than any I'd ever felt before, so cool to the touch of my fingers, of my lips. I slid his shirt back over his shoulders and off. I slid my head down his neck and rested it lightly on his shoulder, as my fingers sought out his nipples. As I touched one, it hardened almost immediately. He grabbed my shoulders, pulling me closer to him. I rolled the tip of the tight skin between my fingers for a moment before moving my head to the nub and taking it into my mouth. (Taking it between my lips is more accurate since there wasn't enough there to suck on.)

Jamie's young body responded as I licked and softly bit at his nipples, urging me on. Taking the hint, I let my right hand slide down his stomach and come to rest at his crotch. He made no effort to push me away. I let my fingers press against him as we lay there kissing and, little by little, I felt him relax against me even as he hardened beneath my touch.

My free hand slipped down and undid his belt and the opening to his jeans. I could sense he was getting a little scared about the whole situation. I comforted him as much as I could with soft whispers that it would be OK. My own cock was straining at my pants. I know he felt it, and honestly I don't really blame him for being a little scared.

"I just want to see you," I whispered. "I won't hurt you. I promise I won't hurt you."

"Okay," he whispered back.

Once his belt and jeans were released it was an easy task to pull them down over his slim hips and legs. His Y-fronts, however, were so damned tight, I don't see how he could breathe. Finally, I slid him out of them and he lay in front of me, nude in the moonlight. I nearly came right then and there as I viewed his young body. He was beautiful. He had a strong little chest, butterfly hips and a smooth flat stomach. The slightest down-like hair had begun to sprout around his pubic area. I guess I stared a moment too long because shyly he pulled me close to him again and kissed me.

I remember watching Jamie's eyes as I undid my own belt

and jeans and let them and my shorts slide down my legs to the ground. His eyes gazed at my enlarged cock and, for the first time that evening, I saw real fright in his face.

"It's okay, Jamie," I whispered. "If it hurts too much, I won't do it. Just tell me and I'll pull out. Okay?"

"Okay."

I had to give it to Jamie Anthony; he was a brave little bugger.

I again let my hand slide down between his legs and let my middle finger probe the crack between his buttocks. This time he didn't press his legs together, in fact, he opened them wider. I reached into the pocket of my trousers and pulled out a tube of Vaseline. Like the good boy scout I'd never been, I was learning to be prepared. Jamie's eyes widened as he watched me unscrew the top, then squeeze out some of the gooey mixture onto my fingers. We used Vaseline for just about everything in school. Maybe it hadn't occurred to the boy that we could use it for this.

I let my gooey finger feel out his unviolated opening, trying to spread his ass lips apart a bit to let my finger enter him. I remember even now thinking that if he was this tight on my finger, how the hell could I get my cock into him? It was time to find out. Edging up between his spread-eagled legs, I heaved them up onto my shoulders. Most of this was guesswork but that seemed the right thing to do. He was a supple little chap and he worked his shoulders around to make himself as comfortable as possible. The look of intense curiosity on his face complemented the look of intense lust on mine.

I let my cock replace my finger at his hot little opening. I pressed insistently and for a moment felt his sphincter give way. I heard Jamie whimper. "It hurts, Tilson, it really hurts." I tried again. I felt Jamie bite into my shoulder, not deep but hard enough to make me wince. I pushed again. This time it wasn't words I heard but muffled sobbing. The boy was trying to hide the pain he was in. As much as I wanted to feel myself inside Jamie, I wasn't prepared to hurt him. I pulled the tip of my cock out of him, lowered his legs and pulled him into my chest. I nuzzled that beautiful dark glossy hair and whispered in his ear. "I don't want to hurt you, Jamie. I'm not going to hurt you. Being with you is enough."

Jamie lapped at my throat with his tongue. Then slid up my face to kiss me almost chastely on the lips. I held him away from me. There were still tears in his eyes. I kissed the bluish skin beneath his eyes and ran the tip of my tongue along those amazing eyelashes. Jamie was smiling now, and that meant more to me than my hot prick up his sweet little ass.

I couldn't resist peering between his legs to see if any damage had been done. His ring was distended, swollen, the lips puffy, but there was no sign of blood. I sighed in relief.

I slid back up Jamie's body, kissed his closed eyes, then let my lips slide down his throat, his chest, his tummy and his light dusting of pubic hair. I slipped his hard prick between my lips. He was sweet and salty. I let him slide all the way in. Soon my head was bobbing over his groin. Occasionally, I'd swallow his balls too. The boy was totally engulfed in me.

His body trembled, shook and shuddered as he spat himself into me in hot little squirts. I held him gently in my mouth until I felt him relax. Then I slid back up his body and kissed him on the lips. His eyes fluttered open. He smiled. I lay on my back beside him and we watched the stars together.

"Look, oh look," cried Jamie, "there's one, crossing Orion, look, a shooting star!"

We watched it cross the sky together and were rewarded by a shower of stars. It was a night to remember.

"I say," said Jamie, after about fifteen minutes, "don't say anything about this to Mike, please. I don't want him to be jealous. He wants to be the first to…you know…"

I cuddled the boy to me. "No, I won't say anything, Jamie. That's a promise."

"And..." Jamie hesitated, reluctant to say what was on his mind.

"Go on, Jamie," I encouraged him. "We have to be able to tell each other everything. Go on."

"Well," the boy said, "You can't do this again. Bugger me, I mean. You can kiss me and suck me and toss me off if you like. And I'd like to do it to you sometimes. But you can't bugger me. Promise?"

I had to ask. "Why not?"

"Because you're far too big. That really hurt. I didn't really enjoy it." He spoke with assured finality. "The sucking and stuff was great. But you're not fucking me and that's that. Okay?"

I pulled Jamie to me and kissed him. "Okay," I agreed. "And no hanging around each other in school. Okay?"

"Oh, I wouldn't do that," chirruped Jamie. "You and Ackerley and Honeyman and Parker are all fucking each other. I'm not getting mixed up in that. I'm nobody's bumchum. Well...," he mused, "maybe I'm Michael's bumchum, but he's mine, too, so that's okay. But we're not getting fucked by you big boys, and that's final."

I was flabbergasted. I rose to my feet, helped Jamie up and dressed him in the dark. He didn't seem to mind. Then he knelt and pulled up my underpants and trousers. He paused and slid my flaccid cock into his mouth. He spat it out. Then he grimaced up at me. "That tastes awful. It tastes like shit!" I laughed and finished dressing. I grabbed him, pulled him to me and kissed his open mouth. "Ugh, you're right," I winced, "it does taste like shit. Let's get back to the disco and grab some cider."

We ran down the hill, hand in hand, Jamie's hair flowing behind him like Ponyboy's mane.

I was unutterably happy, but a little worried, too. Where was all this going to end? The Ram Stam Boys was the name of our band. If it went on like this, it could be the name of our school!

I couldn't have been more prophetic. On Saturday night a howling wind got up. The temperature dropped by fifteen degrees and we woke up to snow flurries on Sunday morning. By lunchtime Miller's Farm was coated with three inches of snow. A lot of the hardier souls decided on an expedition into the wilderness. I declined, intending to curl up with a few Playboys—all right then, a few Playgirls, too, and quietly beat my meat all afternoon. I loved the language I was learning from Playboy and Penthouse; beat my meat, spank my monkey, was a lot more fun that toss myself off, have a wank. Call it what you will. That's what I was going to do.

A better writer than me wrote 'the best laid schemes o' mice and men gang aft agley' but I can confirm the truth of it. I got into what I thought was a silly conversation with Tony Honeyman.

"You couldn't, I bet you couldn't," I argued. "In one afternoon? You must be joking?"

"Go on then. Dare me," grinned Tony. "Just be sure it's a good-looking dare."

And the bet? To seduce a First Year squirt that afternoon. In my mind I riffled through the First Year boys. Why I stopped at Michael Fletcher, I can only guess. Maybe because I was jealous of the time he was spending with Peter Parker. But was I jealous of Michael or jealous of Peter? At any rate, I blurted it out.

"Michael Fletcher."

Tony let out a low wolf whistle. "You know how to pick 'em, Guy boy. Michael Fletcher it is. I bet I can suck his sweet little weenie by four o'clock." I almost blurted out that Michael's weenie, while it was sweet, was by no means little.

"But how will I know if you manage it?" I asked. Tony paused for a moment. "Easy peasy, you can watch. I've never been watched before. The idea's got my dick stirring in my pants."

"But how?"

"You know I've got a single room."

"Yes."

"But it's got bunk beds. You take the top bunk. Get under my duvet. I'll use the couch on the other side of the room." A sudden flashback knocked the breath out of me. Tony, stretched along the four seater couch. Myself kneeling on the carpet. My head bobbing over his crotch. His big prick sliding in and out of my mouth. Was that last year or the year before? Did he have anyone on the upper bunk then? Watching me hone my oral skills on the Headmaster's son?

My stomach felt a bit queasy, but I couldn't back out now. If I did, Tony would only double-dare me, and it would be me on that couch, face down.

"Okay, you're on. When?"

"Give it fifteen minutes. I want to chat to young Fletcher."

"How are you going to get him to spend the afternoon with you?"

Tony winked. "I am the Headmaster's only begotten son. And I'm the only one with a TV that's hooked up to satellite. Trust me, oh ye of little faith." For a moment, Tony sounded uncannily like Dr Moonie.

I winked back. "See ye later, alligator."

We slapped hands, Ram Stam style. "After a while, crocodile."

Back in the room I shared with Peter, I put on a pair of voluminous shorts (all the better to get your hand inside) and an XL T-shirt. Peter was clambering into gear that Scott of the Antarctic would have been proud of. "Sure you aren't coming?" he asked. "Sure, but thanks for the invite. My ankle's still a bit sore. I'm just going to lie here and read my Bible."

"Check out Onan," laughed Peter. I didn't get the reference, but I enjoyed his laughter.

Ten minutes later I was under the duvet on the top bunk in Tony's room. I checked the bed out for creaks. Not a whimper. Tony had been busy with the oil can. What a pro! I felt amazingly silly and amazingly horny. I'd already had one session of voyeurism, that had been accidental. This was planned, premeditated, sneaky, and thrilling.

A few minutes later the door opened and Tony Honeyman ushered in Michael Fletcher. They were both laughing. Like me, they were both in shorts and T-shirts, though neither as baggy as mine. Tony dived on the couch.

"Hey, squirt, flick the tele on. I've got the remote over here." Michael did the job, then threw himself onto the couch. Somewhere beneath me, I heard the tele come to life.

Tony skimmed through the channels. "Yeh, this is the one," he said, "it's only soft-core, but it's better than nothing." Peeping out, I saw Mike nod his head and lick his lips. Ten, fifteen minutes of silence broken only by grunts and heavy breathing from the TV. My prick was like slippery iron in my hand.

I watched Tony stretch his legs out in front of him, aware that the bulge between his legs had to be clearly visible to the boy sitting on the sofa alongside him. They were watching TV, but Tony knew that Mike was keeping one eye on the growing bulge in the older boy's shorts. Mike was sitting with one leg pulled up under him, apparently unaware that the crotch of his white underpants was clearly visible.

Tony leaned back, putting both his arms along the back of the sofa, his right arm behind Mike. Watching the screen, Tony waited a few moments, giving Mike time to get used to having his arm behind him. He let it move down a little, his arm brushing the boy's hair. Mike didn't pull away as

Tony's hand slid slowly down until it rested lightly on the boy's shoulder.

He let his arm come down, encircling Mike's shoulders, his hand resting on the front of the shoulder. Mike seemed to take no notice of this development. Tony moved closer to him, slowly raised his right hand to the lad's cheek and brushed it with his fingertips. This time the younger boy turned his head toward him, looking questioningly at him.

"Honeyman," Mike laughed, "what are you doing?"

"This," Tony replied, kissing him with firm pressure, full on the lips. He pulled back, but the arm around Mike's shoulders and the hand against the side of his face held him lips to lips. The boy's hands came up to his chest to push against him, but gradually, the tension in the boy's arms relaxed as he gave in to a prolonged kiss. The younger boy broke away gasping.

"Why?" he asked.

"Because I want to," he replied. "And by the way, the name's Tony." With that he leaned forward and kissed him again. He worked his lips against the boy's full moist lips. Mike gradually allowed him to open his mouth. Tony brushed his tongue against his front teeth, then gently probed, finding the tip of his tongue with the tip of his. He first toyed with it, and then he gently sucked it between his lips. He continued to kiss Mike, gently working on his tongue with his tongue and lips. Finally, he pulled his head back, breaking the kiss, but leaving his hands on the back of Mike's neck.

"You shouldn't do that," the boy gasped. His face was flushed, and he was breathing heavily.

"I know," Tony replied, kissing him again. As he did so, he slid his hand under Mike's T-shirt and onto his stomach. He reached the waist of his shorts and slid his hand inside the waistband. Mike sighed and opened his legs as Tony brushed through his downy hair and grasped his erection. I could see Michael visibly relax, surrender and give in. He let Tony work his hand down farther between his legs, sliding his finger deeper and deeper into his crack. Finally, he must have had the tip of his finger at the boy's hole. Michael squirmed against Tony's chest. He whispered something, but I could not hear it above the barrage of grunts, moans and wet slapping from the television.

After some time, Tony pulled his finger out and slid his hand back up to the waist of Mike's shorts and underwear. He began inching them down over his hips. The boy was not helping him, but he wasn't resisting either. Maybe he was enjoying the strip-tease of his own body. Finally, Tony got them down far enough to slide them down the rest of the way, and by twisting slightly, he got them over the boy's stockinged feet and off. "God, you're a well-built little fucker," whispered Tony as he manipulated the younger boy's erection. Mike's penis stuck straight out from his body, foreskin drawn back, the head a purplish pink. I could smell him from where I lay; the smell was intoxicating.

With one hand, Tony slid his T-shirt over his head, his shorts to the floor. No underpants. He was naked except for white tennis socks. He tugged at Mike's shirt until both boys were equally naked, spread the length of the couch. Tony slid on top of the boy. He looked down at his face. He lowered himself carefully onto Mike, letting his dick slide down between the boy's legs. His dick was nestled right in the boy's crack, but Mike's bumhole was too far down between his legs to get it in. Tony slid between the boy's legs, then raised them over his own shoulders. As he slid up the boy, Mike's legs and bum were raised from the couch. I saw Tony's left hand slip to the floor and under the couch. One-handed, he brought out a tub of petroleum jelly, school issue. He scooped two fingers full and applied them to the centre of the boy's crack. I heard Mike grunt as a finger penetrated him.

Mike tried to pull away when he felt what Tony was trying to do, but he was in a helpless position, bottom several inches off the couch, legs slung over Tony's shoulders. Pushing slowly and relentlessly, the older boy began to inch his thick swollen prick up the stretching rectum, first the end, then slowly a little of the shaft. Withdrawing a little, he moved forward again. Mike groaned, but did not try to pull away again. Slowly working it in and out, Tony succeeded in getting in a little deeper with each forward thrust. Finally, he had it about three-fourths up the boy's ass. I winced as I watched; I'd felt Tony's prick down my throat a dozen times. I knew how difficult it was to accommodate like that. What must Mike's tiny hole feel like?

Withdrawing again, Tony thrust forward with more force, boring in until his dick was buried to the hilt. From where I watched, I could see the stretched brown ring clasped tightly around the base of the older boy's dick. Withdrawing, Tony thrust forward again, sliding smoothly in up to the hilt.

I stopped working my own swollen prick. I knew a couple more touches would bring me off there and then. I wanted to make it last. To enjoy, even if only vicariously, what my friends were enjoying.

Slowly at first, Tony began to fuck Mike's butt hole, using the full length of his iron-hard dick. The boy began to respond, pushing back to meet his thrusts. His asshole had relaxed to accommodate the huge dick sliding in and out of his greased anus. His eyes were closed but his face revealed the intense joy he was experiencing. Both boys were rocking on the couch, their grunts, squeals and moans harmonising from the fuck symphony on the television. Finally, with a heavy grunt, Tony jammed his dick forward, burying it to the hilt in the spasming sphincter as he shot spurt after spurt of hot cum up the boy's clasping chute.

Finally, they were still, with Tony's dick buried up to the

balls in Mike's bum. Gently, he eased forward, letting Mike's legs slide to the couch, but keeping his dick up the younger boy's rectum. Tangled in their own flesh and sweat, the boys looked beautiful. I was wondering whether or not to climb down and join them when a voice sounded through the room.

"I knew if I left you alone with him for very long, you'd get in his pants, but I never thought you'd get that monster up his ass." Adrian Ackerley, Headboy, was standing in the doorway across the room. He stepped in and closed it behind him.

The boys on the couch froze, their heads twisted towards the door. Then Tony Honeyman spoke. "For fuck's sake, Adrian, you nearly gave me a heart attack." A sweet unbroken, if a little husky voice chimed in. "Me, too, you fucker." There was more going on here than I knew about. How could Michael Fletcher, First Year squirt, lying on a couch with Tony Honeyman's prick up his ass, call the Headboy of the school a 'fucker'? There were mysteries here.

"You two have been formally introduced, I take it," quipped Honeyman.

"Yes, we have," replied Ackerley. "We're both Moonies." That seemed sufficient explanation for Tony, if not for me.

"Just stay right where you are, chaps," Ackerley told the bonded boys as he leisurely stripped off his shirt and shorts. He stepped across the room towards them stroking his dick to erection. Then he dropped to his knees by the couch, feeding his hard-on to Mike's lips. The boy could only get the head of Adrian's cock into his mouth, but he sucked it with the kind of gusto that indicated he'd been there before. Adrian gently stroked the boy's hair while Tony manipulated his hard-on.

Tony must have felt his prick hardening again as he watched Mike's lips slide back and forth on Adrian's prick. Mike apparently felt Tony's cock growing in his ass. Continuing to suck Adrian's prick, he reached back and pushed Tony away, urging him to withdraw from his distended hole. When he was disconnected, Mike pushed Adrian down on his back on the floor, slid from the couch and straddled him. He lowered his dripping hole toward the stiff prick, slowly taking the full length into his cum and jelly filled rectum. When he had the full length buried up him, he leaned forward over Adrian, supporting herself on his outstretched arms and began to screw his ass up and down on Adrian's hard dick.

Tony lay on the sofa and watched for several minutes, stroking his hard-on. Mike glanced at him, seeing that he was still hard. He licked his lips, eyeing the huge boner which the boy was stroking, all the while continuing to fuck himself on Adrian' prick. Tony grinned at him and slid off the sofa, moving around in front of him. From his position under Mike, Adrian watched his fellow Sixth Former rub his huge dick back and forth across Mike's lips, then slip the end into the boy's mouth. Meanwhile, Adrian had slipped his hand between their stomachs and was jacking the youngest boy off in the same rhythm the boy rode him. Without thinking, I adjusted the tempo of my own hand to match what was happening on the floor. I knew I couldn't hold out much longer.

The boys on the floor went off like a controlled explosion. Tony held Michael's head in place as he squirted what cum he had left down the boys throat; Michael bounced up and down on Adrian's prick till his body suddenly froze in rictus. I could see Adrian's buttocks pumping frantically and I knew he was emptying himself into the boy's greasy anus. Adrian's fingers were a blur on Mike's penis which suddenly jetted, jetted and jetted again as his cum flew up the older boy's body, striking him just under the chin three or four times.

As they collapsed into a heap, I went off, too, wrapping the fabric of my shorts round my pumping prick that soaked me with my own cum. If I'd been alone, I'd have screamed in delight. As it was, I jammed a corner of the duvet into my mouth, my legs straight out so that I wouldn't shake the bunks to bits. It felt weird lying there in collapsed silence, the boys on the floor breathing raggedly, and the television grunting and groaning away.

I don't know how long we all lay there. I might have fallen asleep. Then I heard voices. Tony took the lead. "Come on, we can use my private shower. We'd better show ourselves around the place before people start talking."

"Are you going to join Dr Moonie's, Tony?" That was Mike's voice.

"No, I fucking well am not. And it's Honeyman to you, squirt." That was Tony's voice. But it was said in such an affectionate way my anger was quickly quelled.

"And you, Fletcher, should stick to kids your own age." That was Adrian Ackerley. Where had I heard that before?

When I was sure they were gone, I slipped down from the bunk. I turned the TV off. That was a sign to Honeyman I'd actually been there. It meant I'd definitely lost the bet, but it was worth it. Soft core on satellite could never match what I'd witnessed.

Sunday night, our last night, was karaoke night. Dreadful but fun. I sang 'Mad About the Boy', a song we'd learned at home from my mother. I'm not sure who wrote it, but I did it justice that night. I stood in a single spotlight on the darkened stage and sang while Peter played piano. As I sang, I caught the eyes of several boys in the room: Tony Honeyman, Adrian Ackerley, Michael Fletcher, Jamie Anthony and Peter himself. I blushed as I realised for whom I was singing.

Chapter 10

I'd rarely got into trouble at Abertay in my three years there, but two weeks before the Christmas holidays I made up for that by nearly getting expelled.

Kennet was the only town within reasonable distance of school. To walk there by road took around half an hour; crossing the fields cut the trip to about ten minutes. The matter was academic since the town was out of bounds unless specific permission was given, and it was rarely given during the week.

A second obstacle barred our path to town. It was strictly prohibited to cross the fields. In fact, it was prohibited to enter the fields since they were owned by Mr Pirie, a farmer who we understood had no time whatsoever for the school, its staff, or boys. Even in the middle of winter, when it was hard to imagine what damage might be done, Pirie's frozen fields were strictly off limits. Crossing them did not enter my mind until I broke the last bass string on my guitar. No one had a spare, and I was effectively ruled out of rehearsals in the critical few days before the music festival.

On Thursday afternoon, immediately after school, I pulled on my boots, gloves and parka and headed out on my quest. It would take me thirty minutes maximum, there and back. I'd surprise and delight the band by turning up fully stringed. Winter gloom had set in. The chances of being caught were minuscule.

Getting there was easy. Buying the strings was easy. Getting back proved hazardous. I was within three or four minutes of the school when I saw him, and he saw me. It was tricky crossing the frozen ground which occasionally gave way underfoot, ice crackling as my boots slipped into the mud beneath. On the outward journey, I'd noticed a lorry and several complicated-looking pieces of machinery. Drain pipes lay scattered around the lorry. It looked as though Mr Pirie was going to re-drain the whole field.

I'm not sure if Mr Pirie saw me first. His voice suddenly thundered across the field. "Laddie! What do you think you're doing? Come here. I want your name."

I wasn't about to come anywhere and I wasn't about to give him my name. I broke into a trot, my boots sliding on mud and broken ice. Behind me, I heard the voice again. "Oi! Be careful! They're very brittle." I hadn't the faintest idea what he was talking about. I lumbered on.

Beneath me I heard a sudden cracking. I jumped and came down on something that rolled away beneath me, not before the cracking had sounded again, like the report from a starter's pistol. I lost my balance and came down heavily. Crack! There it was again. I staggered to my feet and looked down. My gumboots were surrounded by shards of broken pipe, dull red pipe. Drain pipes! I'd been stomping on Mr Pirie's new drainpipes. In the freezing weather, they'd become brittle, and there I was dancing on them in heavy gumboots.

It was an accident, but I wasn't going to hang around to explain. "You bloody…" That voice again. I stumbled on. I concentrated all my energies on taking a diagonal course without tripping a second time. It was dark by this time, only the lights from the school served as a guide. It was not until I was almost at the bottom of the field that I remembered the stream which divided Mr Pirie's land from school property. I'd missed the bridge. It was too deep to wade across without getting soaked. I didn't want awkward questions back at school. I reached the muddy bank and hesitated. I glanced behind me. The farmer was lumbering towards me out of the gloom. Taking a deep breath, I backed a few paces, then ran forward and leapt. I almost made it!

The freezing water shocked my lungs as I hit it full face.

It was only three or four feet deep; that didn't make it any less cold. I scrambled onto the muddy bank, clawing my way up the steep side. I lay on the top gasping like a landed fish. Behind me, I heard Mr Pirie wading through the stream.

"Are you all right, lad?" He sounded genuinely concerned. I stood up and shook myself like a dog. "You'd better get into school right away. 'Fraid you'll have to give me your name before I let you go." I nodded, mumbled my name, turned and dragged my water-logged carcass towards the school. I staggered into the washrooms in the entrance hall of Main House. Jamie Anthony was there cleaning boots for the senior hockey match on Saturday morning.

"I say, Tilson, you look a bit of a fright. Been fishing?" For a moment I thought he was being funny. I had the urge to put him over my knee, haul down his jeans and spank his bottom. A quick stirring in my loins put paid to that idea. I had other things to do if I was going to survive this adventure.

"No, I slipped up to town," I gasped. "Cross the fields. Got chased by Pirie."

Jamie whistled. "Did he catch you?"

"'Course not! Never got near me," I lied, hoping for the best, fearing the worst. "I trod on some of his pipes." This remark mystified Jamie.

"Phew!" I continued. "I'm not half in a mess." I surveyed myself ruefully in the mirror over the wash basins. "Oh well, I'll clean myself here as best I can, then slip into the showers after Prep. You couldn't get me some towels, Jamie? I don't want to go into the House looking like this."

"Back in a jiffy," chimed Jamie who took off like one of my grandfather's whippets. I stripped to my underwear and splashed hot water over me. The mud ran in rivulets down my face and onto my shoulders. It was quite a job.

Jamie turned up trumps with three huge bathtowels, warm ones, filched from Matron's airing cupboard. I sat down to dry my hair. Jamie, welcome if uninvited, knelt in front of the bench and dried my feet and legs. The washrooms were warm, the towels were warm, and I was beginning to feel human again. A little too human as an erection rose silently in my cotton underpants. I felt Jamie's hand tug them away from my belly. I tried to resist. Honestly. For all of three seconds I tried to resist. With a sigh I gave in and raised my bottom enough for Jamie to slip my underpants beneath me. My hard cock sprang into the air.

I looked down. All I could see was Jamie's thick brown glossy hair. I felt his hot moist mouth close over the head of my cock; the shaft slid all the way in until his lips brushed my pubic hair. I continued toweling my hair. It was a strange but pleasant sensation. I couldn't see the boy's mouth but I felt it round my prick. His warm fingers grasped the base of my shaft and jerked it gently as his lips slid back and forth along its length. I could feel his warm saliva trickle into my hair and down onto my balls. I dropped the towel and looked down.

Jamie had tiny ears. I'd never noticed them before. And his neck slid like a stem of ivory protruding from his dark hair down under his shirt collar. I watched little ripples form in his back as he sucked me. With a great effort, I raised his head from my cock. His eyes were glazed, his lips already red and swollen.

"Don't you like…? Don't you want…?

"'Course I do, Jamie. But not now. We've got less than five minutes before prep. If you want to do that—and, believe me, I want you to do it—I want time to enjoy it." The disappointment fled from the boy's face. He raised his eyebrows and grinned. "Good. I've missed you since…since Miller's Farm, the hill, the shooting stars." I pulled him up into a standing position, my cock against his sweater. "And I've missed you, Jamie Anthony. I want to…"

The prep bell cut us short. Two minute warning. I wrapped a towel around me. "Thanks!" And sprinted for my room. I'd be late. I had to think up an excuse.

In the event, I didn't need one. I'd just finished dressing and combing my hair when Dr Honeyman, the Headmaster himself, stepped into the room. "Tilson. My study. Now."

From his desk he surveyed me grimly in silence for what seemed an eternity. "Well, Tilson, what have you to say for yourself." For a wild moment I wondered whether to try an innocent expression and ask sir what he meant. I decided against it.

"Nothing, sir."

"Nothing? What possible reason can you produce for this wanton destruction? It is beyond my comprehension why any boy—especially a boy with gifts such as your own—should behave in such an extra-ordinary fashion. Not only out of bounds after dark, but trespassing. Not only trespassing but damaging private property. What on earth were you thinking of?"

For a moment I considered explaining that I had to get guitar strings in town. That Ram Stam had to rehearse. That the music competition was only ten days away. But that risked bringing down Dr Honeyman's wrath on the entire trip. Even if I were banned from the trip, I did not want to put it in jeopardy for the others. I said nothing but "Sorry, sir. I know it was stupid, sir."

"But you don't know how stupid it was, Tilson," said the doctor. "I am now going to tell you something that you will keep a secret, an absolute secret. Your word as a gentleman, please." Mystified I gave him my word. "I am going to explain why Pirie Farm is so strictly out of bounds. Sit down, Tilson." I took the seat in front of the desk while sir took the one behind. In spite of my predicament, this was fascinating.

"There is a bomb on Pirie Farm. A very large bomb. An

unexploded bomb."

I sat in stunned silence.

"During the Second World War," said the doctor, "a German Messerschmitt was shot down over Pirie Farm. At that time, the farm belonged to the present owner's grandfather. Before the plane crashed, the pilot released a bomb. He did not survive the crash; the bomb did. It did not explode. It buried itself deeply somewhere on Pirie Farm.

"Although the risk is minimal, it is a risk I cannot take. Therefore, the Pirie family and Abertay School have always agreed to make the entire property out of bounds to boys from this school. In addition, the present Mr Pirie, a thoroughly pleasant fellow with whom I have shared many a dinner, behaves like an ogre towards you boys. You might like to know, he has two sons of his own, and splendid lads they are. Any questions?"

I had a million, but none of them appropriate at that moment. I spoke anyway. "Sir, I realise it was out of order for me to break a school rule. I meant no harm. However, I can't tell you why I needed to get to town so desperately. I did not mean to break any of Mr Pirie's drain pipes. I didn't see them until it was too late. I would like to apologise. And I am prepared to accept my punishment, whatever it is." For me that was quite a speech, but I was desperate.

"Good," smiled Dr Honeyman. "That's what I hoped to hear. I have spoken to Bill Pirie on the telephone. He has agreed to accept your apology, and my terms for your punishment."

I gulped.

"Immediately after classes on Saturday, that is to say at 12.30, I will drive you to Pirie Farm. You will work under Mr Pirie's direction all Saturday afternoon and all Sunday. In that way, you will pay your debt to Mr Pirie, to the school, and to society. Are we agreed?" He stood up.

I stood up. He extended his hand. "I agree, sir," I said. We shook hands. "And thank you, sir."

"No, don't thank me, Tilson. Thank Mr Pirie. And thank Tony Honeyman, too." My puzzlement showed.

"Tony explained to me about the strings. You know how persuasive my son can be. But only once, Tilson, only once." I nodded. "And, Tilson, before you go, would you like to explain to me the significance of Ram Stam? I fail to comprehend the reference."

I explained the origin of The Ram Stam Boys.

"Very imaginative, Tilson. Very imaginative. That's what I like my boys to be, original and imaginative. Now get to Prep, and get an early night. I imagine you're going to need it."

"Good night, sir."

"And Tilson..."

"Yes, sir?"

"Wipe the mud from behind your ears. You are fifteen, you know."

"Yes, sir. Thank you, sir."

Saturday afternoon came with a rush. For the first two hours I spent my time helping with the drainage of the meadow, mostly acting as general gofer for the men. It was: "Boy! This pipe is cracked. Bring another from over there." Or: "Boy! Ask the boss to let us have the machine over here. We'll have to go a bit deeper." Or: "Boy! Get the kettle on."

That job finished, I was employed at the farm itself. Mr Pirie was having some repair jobs done, and once again my work was mainly fetching, carrying, and taking messages, but I was also allowed to help with painting and creosoting. Mr Pirie was surprisingly pleasant, considering the damage I'd done. He gave me a quiet word of greeting when I arrived and a word of thanks when each job was finished, but I suspected that he was keeping an eye on me and that he would have spotted at once if I'd started to slack. Not that I had any intention of slacking once I got into the work. It was very satisfying to see real jobs completed.

At the end of the afternoon, Mr Pirie called me over. "Well, lad," he said, "you've put in a good afternoon's work. Tomorrow's Sunday so we won't be laying drain pipes. How about working in the granary? It's pretty heavy work, but I think you're up to it." I nodded and blew into my hands. Working outside had frozen me stiff.

The farmer laughed good-naturedly. "At least you'll be warm in the granary. You'll be stacking hay with Dan. We've got to keep the hay absolutely dry, so we keep the central heating well up. You won't need a sweater I can tell you that. Be here at ten sharp."

"Yes, sir," I said, "and sir...I'm sorry for the damage I did. I really didn't mean it."

"I didn't think you did, Mr Tilson, but we've all got to pay our dues." He shook my hand which I thought was jolly decent of him. I headed home with a far lighter heart.

Back in school I had dinner and a hot shower. I fended off questions from Peter and Tony. Frankly I was exhausted but it was a good feeling. Once again, my room mate had gone home for the weekend; he might just as well have been a weekly boarder. I didn't mind. I watched a bit of TV, then headed for bed, knowing I was going to be working very hard all of Sunday. I didn't mind. In fact, I was quite looking forward to it.

I'd just slipped into bed and was reading by lamplight—I can't sleep unless I read something, anything first—when the door slipped open and shut. A slim figure bounded across the room and leapt onto my bed. It was Jamie! He, too, was in pyjamas.

"Please don't throw me out," he whispered. "Tell me about the farm." I recalled how helpful the boy had been when I arrived wet, muddy and bedraggled. He was one of the few people who knew why I'd 'disappeared' on Saturday afternoon. Jamie deserved to know.

I pulled aside my duvet and he snuggled under. I was in enough hot water already; I didn't want to be discovered with a First Year on my bed. "Anybody knocks, dive under the duvet," I whispered. Jamie giggled, "That's what I'm going to do anyway. And besides, Ackerley and Honeyman are on duty." No further elaboration was required. I gave Jamie a detailed account of my day down on the farm. He seemed fascinated by everything I had to tell him. Finally, I lay back, with his head in the crook of my arm, his big brown eyes gazing up at me. Get thee behind me, temptation, but it never did. At least on this occasion it wasn't I who made the first move. That's not quite true. I was already stroking Jamie's prick; it raised his pyjama bottoms like a little tent pole.

"Look here," Jamie said, reaching into the back pocket of his pyjamas. "I've brought you a present." He pulled out a familiar tub of Vaseline. I wondered if Matron had any left in her cupboard in surgery.

"Vaseline?" I said.

"You don't like it," he said, sounding hurt.

"No, I'm just surprised. You know what it's used for, don't you? And I'm not talking about cuts and grazes."

"I'm not simple, you know," giggled Jamie. "I'm not having your big prick up me without something to help. We've already tried that. My bumhole still itches."

I stroked his hair and kissed his lips, nose, and forehead. "What about that promise I made to you before, that I would never fuck your ass? Is that still binding?"

"Does it look like it?" Jamie smiled, indicating the Vaseline.

"I promise. If it hurts, just say so and I'll stop."

"You want me to suck you off first?" Jamie asked in all seriousness. "That way, you won't be so hot?"

"I think I can control myself," I murmured. What can you say about a boy like that? His thoughtfulness showed the real spirit of the public school through the ages.

I drew him to me and slid his pyjamas to his knees. His penis, when I touched it, was stiff, his balls riding high in their sockets. I slid my finger up and down his slit. Jamie moaned and bobbed his hips in time to my finger.

"You're so sweet to let me do this," I said. "I want you to be happy," he said. "You make me happy," I said, sliding his pyjamas all the way off. His top quickly followed, my own pyjamas landing on them in a crumpled heap.

I turned him over and, cupping his ass in my hands, began to lick his hole. A man-cub. A delicious man-cub. (We did *The Jungle Book* at my junior school.) The sweet, puckered slit seemed to puff up under my lips. Holding his buttocks apart, I stroked his ring with my tongue, spitting into the cavity and letting my saliva slide in there, too. Jamie made a series of high-pitched squeaks and squeals. I didn't worry about us being overheard; it would have taken a finally-tuned bat detector to have picked them up.

I worked a finger deeper into his hole, past the muscle. I slid it back and forth in time with my tongue that stroked the soft smooth skin inside his thighs. He began to buck. "Oh, Guy, Guy…" he whispered. I put some jelly on my finger and touched his hole. He jumped. "It's cold."

"Not for long." I slid it all over the hole, then pushed my middle finger inside. Lubricated by the Vaseline and by our previous playing, it slipped deep inside. After a few minutes, I added a second finger that slid in to the hilt. Jamie was moaning audibly, but there was more pleasure than pain in the sounds.

I took my fingers out and smeared Vaseline the length of my cock. I turned Jamie on his back and lifted his legs over my shoulders, raising his bum to my crotch. I pressed down the shaft of my erection until the head was firmly against his greasy hole. I looked down into those deep pools of liquid brown. Jamie looked back at me, a smile trembling on his lips. He shivered and pushed back on my cock. It took a little working, but the head suddenly popped past the sphincter into his bottom. I paused to let him get used to the feel, then, spreading his cheeks wider, rammed my cock in deeper. It hit the muscle and he jumped.

"It hurts," he whispered.

"Just relax. I'm not going any further till you're ready. Just relax and get used to the feeling." I stroked his chest, his nipples, his tummy, his belly, gently jacked his cock. I kissed his neck and he arched. "Mmm," he said. I slid my cock deeper into his rectum. He gasped, then I popped the ring of his ass muscle wide open and my cock slid in to the hilt, my pubic hair brushing against his cheeks. I was in Jamie's ass. The thought nearly made me shoot my load.

"I'll wait," I said. "Just relax and it'll be fine." He rocked slowly back and forth, my cock sliding in and out at the tempo he set.

"Don't move," he said, "I want to try something." He curled up tight, making his ass open and grab my cock. His cheeks touched my body. "That's it," I whispered. "That's as far as it goes." The boy started rocking on my cock, squeezing his ass cheeks. His breath started to come in ragged gulps.

"Guy," he whispered, "do it, fuck me rotten." I started rocking in time to his own rhythm. God, he was hot and tight. His anal ring was distended like a tight elastic round my shaft.

"Do it," he whispered, "do it right up my bum."

"I will. Oh, yes, like that..."

"Yes, all the way up," he moaned.

"I'll cum with you," I said, tossing him off ruthlessly.

"Yes..." I could feel his stiffen. "Now," he said, the word coming calmly, slow and distinct.

I masturbated him furiously. "Guy...I'm...going...to..." He squeezed my cock so hard I thought he'd 'bite it off' at the base. I felt the cum race up my shaft. With a violent shudder, he pushed back on my cock. His cheeks squeezed and squeezed. His body shuddered with wave after wave of cumming. My own orgasm started to rise and, blind with frenzy, I pumped into his ass again and again. The force was so strong, I felt it shoot back against me, leaking around my cock and out of his asshole.

We collapsed that way, my cock throbbing, Jamie's buttocks clenching and unclenching for a long time. We both shivered as the waves of our orgasms subsided. Finally, it was over. He twisted, and my cock slid out of his ass, covered by sloppy cum, Vaseline, and brown juices. As I collapsed on to him, I felt and heard his cum squelch between us. We both giggled.

"That was nice, Guy," he said. "It really was."

"I'm glad. I loved it. Did it hurt?"

"Yes, but I'm glad I did it for you."

I pulled this lovely boy to me. "You know, it's not only the sex, Jamie. I really like you, I really do. I only wish..."

Jamie silenced me with a touch of his lips. "I know. I wish the same."

"What?"

"I wish we were in the same year," he said. "Then it wouldn't be so difficult to get together." This boy was a mind-reader as well as a hot little fuck.

"Then you'd be able to stay the night," I said. "We'd be able to sleep together."

Jamie snuggled into me and nibbled the hair in the left armpit. "At least we can do that tonight?"

"What?" I asked.

"I can sleep here tonight," he said, "with you."

"No you can't..." I began to protest. He kissed me on the

lips again. "Yes, I can. Ackerley and Honeyman saw me coming in here, in pyjamas. And you know what?"

"What?"

"Ackerley slapped my ass. Honeyman wished me 'good luck'."

It was my turn to kiss Jamie.

"Have you got a watch?" he asked.

"Yes, why?"

"So you can set the alarm for one hour," he said.

"Why?" I asked. My orgasm must have killed a few million brain cells.

"Well," Jamie explained patiently, "after a little sleep, the alarm will wake us up, and I've still got plenty of Vaseline left."

This time when we kissed our mouths were open, and our tongues probing those places where only the dentist's drill had gone before. Jamie wound his legs around me. I felt his cock mash against my balls, my hair tickle his tummy. If it turned out I was a paedophile, I'd never find another boy as lovely to paedophile with than Jamie Anthony.

"Mmmmmm…"

"Mmmmmmm…"

"Mmmmmmmmmm…!"

In the morning we woke early and Jamie slipped into the showers before anyone else was up and about. I waited fifteen minutes. To tell the truth, I wasn't sure that I could resist Jamie's lithe little body awash with hot water and soapy bubbles. I also wanted to conserve my energy for what Farmer Pirie promised would be a hard day.

Chapter 11

I arrived at the farm just after nine. Pirie gruffly but warmly directed me to the granary which lay half a mile from the main farm buildings. "Dan's expecting you. I'll have your lunch sent around one o'clock." He chuckled. "I hope you've strength enough left to eat it."

As soon as I entered the granary, a wave of heat washed over me. "Close that door," a voice shouted. A young man came over and introduced himself as Dan, my boss for the day. He shook my hand. His grip was dry and friendly.

"You must be Guy Tilson," he said and grinned. "The naughty boy. Well, don't worry, I like naughty boys. Nothing worse than a dull youngster." This sounded a little odd from a young man who couldn't have been that much older than me. If I'd had to guess his age, I'd have said twenty-five, twenty-eight, but he addressed me as if he were years older than that.

"Yes, sir," I said.

"Less of the 'sir'. You're Guy. I'm Dan. What I say goes? Right, Guy." It was my turn to grin. "Right, Dan." He showed me where to hang my anorak. I exchanged my gumboots for light canvas slip-ons.

"First job is to shovel that loose grain back into a granary cone," Dan explained. "Here's your shovel. Mind you don't fall in. You do, and you won't be coming out in a hurry." My little Adam's apple bobbed a bit.

We climbed the ladders up the side of a gleaming cone. On either side there was a platform. Behind each platform was a huge metal bin. I watched Dan slide the latch on his bin, then slide the latch on mine. Grain whooshed out like fast-flowing lava down a mountainside. Within seconds I was up to the knees in it. Dan threw a switch and the top of the cone slid back. He began to shovel in the grain. I watched and copied what he did. It was easy, it was fun.

It was easy and fun for about twenty minutes. Then my shoulders began to ache. Then my back, Then the top of my buttocks. Sweat was streaming down my face.

"Hey, Guy," called Dan from the other side, "slow down. Don't try to keep up with me. Find your own pace and stick to it." I was a little embarrassed but I wasn't stupid. I slowed down until I found an easier rhythm, swinging the shovel back and forward like a plectrum over guitar strings. Like most physical things, it was matter of technique, of finding the knack. I found I was pushing the grain just as much as lifting it; that made it a whole lot easier. As I shoveled, grain kept on sliding out of the bin in what seemed a never-ending stream. Finally the stream trickled and died. Finally my platform was clear.

I looked over at Dan. He was sitting on the platform, legs dangling into the cone, humming a tune I might have recognised if it hadn't been so off-key. He'd stripped to his waist. I'd been so busy concentrating on my own work, I hadn't noticed. I wished I had. My T-shirt and the backside of my jeans were soaking. My hair hung in damp clumps around my ears. So much sweat had dried on my face I could taste salt on my lips. I had a few moments to study Dan before he noticed I was finished.

He was well-built, slim but with powerful shoulders. He'd done a lot of heavy work in his time. He was olive-skinned, testifying to a summer spent stripped and outdoors. His hair was raven-black, thick and glossy. His skin was so clear that it was hard to guess his age. Around 30 tops, I thought. His eyes were spread apart with thick eyebrows that almost met in the middle. A strong nose and high cheekbones excused the rather full and pouty lips. Something about Dan was disturbingly familiar. He raised one arm and scratched at his back, just below his neck. Thick black hair filled his armpits, though curiously enough his finely-muscled chest was hairless. A fine line of black hair ran from his navel and disappeared under the waistband of his jeans. I realised I was staring. I realised I was getting a hard-on. This full-grown man, sitting semi-naked and unaware, was giving me an erection. I coughed and scuffed my feet along the platform.

Dan turned. "Finished already? Strong little bugger, you are, Guy Tilson. Let's get down and have a couple of drinks. You need them in this heat."

I scrambled down the ladder, surreptitiously maneuvering my hard-on straight up my belly. On the granary floor, Dan pulled over a few sacks and organised them like a set of bean bags. "Sprawl there," he said before disappearing into a small office. He returned with four bottles of beer, continental style, and opened a couple of them.

"Here," he said, "you're too young to drink beer, so it'll taste all the better." I took a swig, coughed, spluttered and lost some of the beer through my nose. Dan laughed. He had a penetrating sort of laugh, rather like water gurgling down a drain. "Stop gulping. Take it in easy, you'll enjoy it all the more." Dan sprawled beside me. "And get that T-shirt off. You're starting to stink like last week's laundry."

His humour made me grin. I slid off the shirt with difficulty as it stuck to my back. Dan reached over and helped me, his huge fingers brushing my bare skin and making me shiver. "Now tell me about this school of yours."

"What would you like to know?"

"Everything," he said and leaned back, the neck of the bottle between his lips. I told him whatever came into my head. Dan was a good listener. He asked just enough questions to prompt me when I dried up. He seemed genuinely curious, genuinely interested. By the end of my second beer, I was thoroughly relaxed, though my shoulders ached a bit. I must have winced for Dan suddenly switched position, sitting himself behind me, legs stretched out on either side of me, and began to massage my shoulders, his thumbs gently working the knots in my upper back. The sensation was as relaxing as the beer.

My words were replaced by a comfortable silence. His hands worked my shoulders, my neck, the small of my back. They slid around front and his fingers criss-crossed my chest in a light massage, his thumbs brushing my nipples. It must have been the beer; I felt neither scared nor embarrassed. Even when his hands slid lower and caressed my stomach, my hips, my belly button, and his fingers slid into the little gaps at top of my jeans, it seemed the most natural thing in the world.

"And what do you do for sex?" came the voice in my ear. "There can't be many girls about an all boys' school. So how do you cope?" The palm of one hand slid over my crotch, his fingers closing round my hard-on. "Is this okay for you?" the voice whispered in my ear. I leaned back into his chest. "Yes," I said, my voice leaping an octave halfway through the word.

Dan continued to stroke me. I leaned against his chest and drank in the smells of the first man who'd ever touched me sexually. He held the tip of his beer bottle against my lips. I let him slide the bottle in and tilt it. I guzzled at the beer, already wondering what his cock would taste like. Not a boy's cock, a real man's cock. My erection was so hard it ached. I shifted position so that Dan could maneuver my prick around and get a real grip of it.

My penis throbbed with pleasure as he held it between his thumb and forefinger through my trousers. It grew harder as he fondled it. My breathing came more quickly now, and I twisted to see him smiling at me.

"I want to see you naked," he whispered as he nuzzled my right ear.

I lay back against him, kicked off my slip-ons and wriggled out of jeans and underpants. It was weird to lie there naked in the arms of a man, but something felt right about it. I could feel a bulge in his denims press into my lower back. I yearned to feel his nakedness against mine as I watched his huge right hand play with my fully erect penis. Dan turned me round so I lay along his body, my stiff cock pressed against his hot bulge. His arms enfolded me, and we kissed a long probing kiss. I'd never kissed a man that way before; it was wonderful! I matched every movement of his tongue in my mouth with a response from my own tongue.

My left hand dropped to the lump in his pants. It felt huge! Much bigger than my own boy's penis. I had to know what it was like. I squeezed the living flesh beneath my fingers.

"Mmmm!" Dan murmured. "You public school boys are always hot! I like that. Come on!"

He stood and pulled me to my feet. Standing, he took me in his arms for some more kissing and feeling. I could feel the hardness of his cock pressing into my naked thigh through his pants. I couldn't wait any longer. I slid down his body. Kneeling, I opened the buckle on his belt and unzipped him. His hard, tight buttocks made it difficult for me to wrestle his jeans down his legs, but I was adamant. I wanted to see him, touch him, smell him, taste him. At last his jeans and shorts were in a crumpled heap round his ankles.

I got my first good look at his cock which stuck proudly out from a forest of curly black hair in his groin. The same hair ran up the inside of his legs and disappeared into his crack. Even the underside of his balls were hairy, which made him so manly compared to my hairless nuts. He had the most wonderful cock I'd ever seen. About eight inches long, its straight thick shaft ended in a beautifully circumcised head. Dan's was my first circumcised penis. I knelt there in awe and wonder. I ran my hand along his stomach, almost afraid to touch the treasure below in case he pushed my hand away.

I moved my hand a little further down, and felt the first brush of his pubic hair under my fingertips. I played with my fingers in his curly black bush causing Dan to writhe a bit with pleasure. I wanted so much to touch him. So much to feel him. To hold it in my hands, press it against my face and lips, to get to know every inch of it. I knew that I had to do it. I mustered all of my courage, and my hand moved lower. My hand touched Dan's cock! A shiver of pleasure ran through me, and Dan moaned in ecstasy, his hands running through my hair, then pressing my face closer to his huge horse cock, his low-hanging balls, and his thick curly bush.

Dan let me play with his cock for a long time, almost like a dad teaching his son how to drive, with patience, tolerance and not a little humour. I ran my fingers all over his cock, and rolled the shaft between my palms. I weighed his balls in my hands, and gently kneaded his scrotum. I let myself be guided by what I knew I liked to have done to me, and by my desire to explore all of this man. I was absorbed in the experience. This is what I wanted! This is what I was made for!

I heard Dan growl into my ear with an urgency I'd never heard from anyone. "I want you—now!" He sank down onto the sacks and pulled me with him. Gripping me tightly, he rolled me onto my stomach over a sack of grain. I felt exposed, vulnerable, utterly open to his touch, his gaze, to whatever he wanted to do to me. And whatever he wanted to do, that's what I wanted done to me.

"Hold still!" he ordered, and I felt a warm lump of grease squirt onto my asshole. I flinched at first, then wiggled my ass as I felt Dan's fingers rub the jelly into my anus. One finger, two, then three probed and penetrated me. It hurt like Hell! Dan's hand was in the space beneath me. His fingers jacked my aching erection. I couldn't make up my mind which I felt more: the pain or the pleasure. I didn't care; the pain was part of the pleasure.

Then there was something other than fingers at my asshole. I immediately knew what it was. I let out a small prayer that I could take enough of Dan to satisfy him. I felt Dan push at my tender, bottom and felt my flesh spread and give way as he forced his way deep inside of me! I felt as if I was being impaled on an enormous hot rod as my asshole spread wider and wider to accept him into me. It hurt! Jesus H. Christ, it hurt, like nothing I'd ever felt hurting before, but it felt so good, so very good at the same time. The spasms of pain rippled through me, but soon subsided to a level that I could handle. I rode along with the ripples of pleasure that coursed through my throbbing penis and my throbbing rectum. This was what I'd wanted, and now I was getting it. If this was the life of a farmer's boy, give it to me—eight days a week!

Dan rode me for a long time, sometimes sweet, sometimes rough, sometimes slow, sometimes fast, sometimes gently, sometimes brutally, matching the strokes up my ass with the strokes around my hot, greasy, sweating, raw prick. I reveled in every stroke, and gasped in ecstasy every time he drove that wonderful cock of his into me.

I wanted it to go on for ever, but then there was something different in Dan. His movements became erratic, and his body stiffened noticeably. He drove his cock deep into my bowels with a violence I hadn't felt from him before. He groaned a deep guttural growl, and I felt the heat of his cum filling me! That was the signal. My cock swelled in his hand, throbbed, pulsated and shot great gobs of cum somewhere below me. I rocked out of control under his body as he rocked on top of mine. We were glued together, by lust, desire, semen, sperm, cum, sweat, and sheer fucking fun.

After what seemed like an eternity, Dan pulled himself out, still half erect, and rolled away from me. I turned, slid off the sack and lay on my back, my cock at half mast above my groin. Dan pulled me into him and cuddled me in his arms; our sweaty, half-tumescent pricks rubbed against each other, so sensitive that it hurt. "Okay, Guy?" he whispered. "Okay, Dan." He reached behind him and pulled out an open bottle of beer from a private stash. He pushed me back from him and let the beer run down my chest, tummy and swollen penis. The beer was ice-cold. My bottom leapt a foot off the granary floor.

Dan laughed and bent over me. "This is the way I like my beer," he said and lapped it up from my chest, licking me all over as he scooped the liquid and my cum into his mouth. His lips touched the head of my cock. I pulled back as if I'd been stung. "Still sensitive, huh," he said. I took the bottle from his hand and poured it over his cock. It was Dan's turn to wince. I leaned over him and took the head of his cock into my mouth; that was all I could manage. It was a weird mixture of tastes and smells, but there was something magical about it.

"Essence of Man" is what I thought, and I decided there and then to try and write a song about it for The Ram Stam Boys. Of course, I'd disguise what it really meant and I wouldn't reveal the source of my inspiration. This man's cock, his taste, his smell, his cum up my arse was mine!

I'd tried my hand at song-writing before but Tony'd been none too impressed. Like everyone else, I was shocked by the death of Princess Diana, and moved by Elton John's 'Wind' in the Cathedral. I thought I'd have a go at writing a tribute from the band. It began: "You were loved everywhere you went, You let retarded people lick your face." Tony vetoed it before I even got the third line out! I never understood why.

We lay there for a while saying nothing. I drank in the smells and listened to the hum of the dynamo. I must have fallen asleep in his arms. He was shaking me gently. "C'mon,

Tiger, we've got work to do." Sleepily, I let him haul me up to my feet. I stood there like a three-year-old as he dressed me. The beer made me feel snoozy and groggy. Dan lifted me up by the legs and swung me around till I was upside down in his arms, feet in the air, hair brushing the granary floor. He held in one arm and tickled me with his free hand. I couldn't stop laughing and the laughter shook the sleep out of me.

"That's how I get my son awake," he said switching me round effortlessly and lowering me to the floor. My mouth must have dropped. Dan had a son. He laughed and ruffled my hair. "Just because I like sex with boys doesn't mean I can't have one of my own. I like sex with men and women, too. It takes all kinds of people to make the world go round." I popped this mystery on the mental back burner to await more leisurely inspection.

"Right, shifting bales time," Dan said. "We've got to move that section of hay over to the entrance. There's a pick-up tomorrow." My Adam's apple must have bobbed again. "No, we're not doing it by hand. At least you're not." He indicated a yellow fork-lift truck. "I'm going to teach you to operate that truck. I'll load, you drive. Drop a single bale and your ass is mine." I grinned. "No, I don't mean for that. I mean for a regular big-time spanking."

The next couple of hours were great. After fifteen minutes, I got the hang of the fork lift. Dan loaded the bales, I drove them to the entrance station, tilted the forks and let them slide off, returned and picked up my next load. After half a dozen loads, Dan came over and piled them high. Though he didn't look over-muscular, he was incredibly strong, tossing around the bales as if they were duvets. I wondered if I'd ever have muscles like Dan's…or a horse cock like his.

Around lunchtime, Molly arrived from the farmhouse with two platters piled high with grub. Steaks, french fries, strawberries and ice cream. Dan magicked a couple more beers from the office fridge. This was it: a farmer's life for me. All this grub and a hot cock up my ass. What boy could ask for more?

Mr Pirie came in. He ignored me. I sensed rather than saw his smile. I lay against a bale, glassy-eyed and burping politely. He looked around the granary and gave a low whistle of approval. He had a quiet word with Dan and left.

Dan sat down on a bale next to mine. "Mr Pirie says a couple of hours more should do it. He'll pick you up at three and drive you back to the school. He didn't say so, but he's pleased. So am I."

I hauled myself up. "What've we got to do? Let's get started now."

"What for?" Dan asked. "There's only about an hour's work. No hurry."

"Yes, there is. Start now and we'll have an hour to kill." I raised my beer bottle and slid the neck between my lips. I pumped it slowly back and forwards into my mouth. Dan grinned. "Fucking teenagers. Wish I was fifteen again."

We worked hard for the next hour, shoveling grain from the main silo into smaller aluminium holders. Off came the shirts again. I sweated out most of the beer that ran down my back in small rivers. Once or twice Dan made a grab for me. I giggled as he licked the beer between my shoulder blades and down the small of my back. Finally, the work was done. We packed away the shovels. Dan called me into the office.

There was a bed, a big one, almost a double bed, low slung, almost touching the floor. Dan explained. "At harvest time there's so much work that guys on shift work round the clock, two at a time. The non-working pair kip down on this bed. Usually all they do is sleep. Seems a bit of a waste." He grabbed me and slung me down on the bed, stretching me out so that I was spread-eagled above him. "Well, Tiger, we've got an hour."

Maybe I hadn't sweated out all of the beer because suddenly I didn't give a fuck. I went with my instincts, no matter how childish they seemed. I lowered my head to his chest and began running my tongue around his nipples. They seemed to swell and grow under my touch until the centres stuck out like little brown mountains on a rosy plain. Experimentally, I drew a nipple into my mouth and began to suck on it. It was amazingly satisfying. The pressure of Dan's hands around my head increased as I tried to suck as much of him into my mouth as I could. Then I began running my tongue down his chest to his stomach and back to his chest. I was curious to see how far I could tease him.

Taking his louder moans for permission, I undid his jeans. He lifted his ass and helped me slide them down and off. I began to go lower toward his cock. He pulled my head away, looked into my eyes, and whispered, "Do you know what you're doing?" I nodded and lowered my head to his stomach again. I ran my tongue around the area, occasionally dipping below his underpants. Finally in desperation, I grabbed them and roughly hauled them off. His thick prick, huge balls and black curly forest lay open to my gaze and my mouth.

Starting at his knees, I ran my tongue up his legs to where his hairs started tickling my nose. I guessed I should start at his cockhead because that's where I was always most sensitive, and anyway his thick shaft, that looked seven or eight inches long and a couple of inches round, scared me a bit. It was amazing to think I'd taken this 'truncheon' up my arse.

I sucked as much of his prick as I could manage deep into my mouth. My lips were stretched round his shaft. Dan arched his hips. Whatever I lacked in experience I tried to make up for in effort. I kept sucking fiercely, my saliva mixing with his juices until he was soaked. Leaving his cock, I moved down and nuzzled into the crack between his buttocks. He swung his legs up until they were wrapped around my ears.

Taking a deep breath, I shoved my tongue as far into his shithole as it would go.

He mashed my head against him moaning, "Jesus fuck… Holy shit… Mother of god…" and similar exhortations. He was obviously a Catholic. I began thrusting my tongue in and out with short trips back up to his thick-veined, sweaty cock.

Dan's moaning turned me on even more and made me determined to give him as much pleasure as he had given me. It was great to be fifteen and in control of a fully-grown man.

I tried to get more of him down my throat but I gagged and choked. He pulled my head away carefully. I was feverishly excited and capable of anything. Dan smiled knowingly at me and lay back down, spreading his legs and maneuvering me between them. This was it. The moment of truth!

I knelt between his legs. He reached down and grabbed my cock. I almost fainted. Just having Dan touch my cock was fantastic. Grabbing my swollen penis, he pulled me towards him and down to his asshole. Without letting go of my cock, he slowly worked it into his sphincter. Grabbing my ass with his other hand, he pushed me into him. I couldn't believe the sensation! When he had all of me inside him, he let go of my cock, grabbed my ass with both hands, and moved his hips up and down against me in a rippling motion. I was fucking a man! I got carried away and thrust with all my might into him, his hands on my ass pulling me deeper into his rectum. I drove in and pulled out as hard and fast as I could, then drove home again. The ring of his hole ran tightly the length of my cock, spurring me on to in-and-out even faster. I could hear sticky, slappy, wet sounds as my body glued to his for a moment, then was pulled away again. The sounds, the smells, the sensations drove me on till I was humping like a mad thing.

I couldn't take much more. Feeling an orgasm start, I shouted, "Dan! Dan!" Too late, I started shooting inside him, my butt bouncing up and down between his hairy legs. I leaned on my arms, propping myself up so I could look into his eyes as I shot my load. Dan didn't blink. He was almost solemn, like some parent animal watching its young learn the tricks of survival. Sweat flew from my hair into his face and eyes; he didn't blink once. My whole groin felt as if it were melting, melting into my prick and shooting itself up this man's hot, hairy ass. I wondered what my hard prick, small compared to Dan's cock, looked like in that dark, meaty, juicy cavern.

Smiling, he stroked my cheek and asked, "Do you want to stop?" I shook my head fiercely and started stroking my still hard cock inside him. Now I understood one of the benefits of being 15, healthy, and horny as Hell: once wasn't going to be enough! I also noticed that my first orgasm seemed to deaden the sensations in my cock. Realizing I could now fuck him without worrying about cumming too fast, I went at it with renewed teenage gusto.

Dan looked at me and moaned, "I don't believe it!" My ego soared! I was Cheetah dominating Tarzan! I was the fulfilment of the male image! Marlboro Man, look out! I'm riding this colt into the sunset! I kept up the pace, going in and out, as deep as I could, Dan writhing and moaning, driving me to animal passion that scared me. His hips thrust back at me and met my every stroke with equal passion. Suddenly, he grabbed me around the hips with his legs, and, sinking his teeth lightly into my neck, began to cum. His ring clamped down on my cock and I could feel it pulsate in rhythm to convulsions that had me bouncing in his crotch.

That set me off. I was lost in the throes of his orgasm and mine. As we shot our loads, I couldn't believe that I'd actually done it to a man! I bet even Tony hadn't done that yet. Another thing I couldn't believe: my cock was as hard as ever. I withdrew it a little sheepishly from his hole. Dan looked down at it and smiled. "You damned teenagers. That's what I like about you. You can never get enough."

Using both hands he gently forced me away until I was lying on my back. Dan began running his tongue down my legs and around my stomach, careful to avoid my erection. I moaned and writhed under his ministrations, thrusting my hips involuntarily into the air. At last, he began tonguing my balls. He went back and forth between them, soaking with his saliva. He took my left testicle into his mouth. He sucked on it softly and stroked it with his tongue. Letting it slide sensuously out of his mouth, he replaced it with the right testicle. He went back and forth between them, using his mouth to 'fuck' my balls, sliding them individually in and out, in and out. Taking a deep breath, he took both balls into his mouth, sucked on them and rolled them around with his tongue. The sensation was overwhelming. My cock felt more engorged with blood than ever, bouncing up at the granary roof with every beat of my heart. I felt as stiff and rigid as the silo we'd been filling.

Suddenly, he pulled back and let my balls pop out of his mouth. He began running his tongue up and down on the underside of my cock. Occasionally he would wrap his lips around the side of my cock and suck it or stroke his lips up and down, pausing close to the head. He opened his mouth and placed my cock inside on his tongue, rubbing it all around without closing his mouth. It was almost unbearable.

Dan grabbed my cock and closed his mouth about the head, slowly sucking it in until he had most of it in his mouth. He kept it there, sucking on it like a lollipop, his eyes glued to mine, savouring my every reaction. He closed his eyes and started stroking his head up and down on my bursting penis, going deeper and deeper with every stroke, until finally all of my cock was buried in his mouth and his lips ground into my curlies. I could feel my balls swelling, getting ready to expel my juices for the fourth time that day.

I grabbed his head and started helping him up and down on my cock. The pressure kept increasing and increasing until suddenly, I began to cum! Jet after jet spurted into his throat. I couldn't stop spurting; Dan couldn't get enough. As the flow lessened, he pulled his head back and began running my dripping cock around his face. The muscles in my body were shaking from the tension.

Finally he took my softening cock back into his mouth, gently licking and sucking it. He used his fingers to wipe off his face and sucked my semen from his lips. Then he reached for me and took me in his arms. It felt like coming home.

I tried to snuggle down to some sleep, but Dan shook me, whispering, "Not this time, Tiger. It's quarter to three. We don't want to get caught with our pants down." We got up. Dan found some hankies, cleaned ourselves up as much as we could, then dressed. We went back into the granary and sat on some of the bales we had stacked.

"Dan, can I come back again—to help you, I mean?"

He held my face between his huge fingers. "'Fraid not, Tiger. I'm going back tomorrow."

My heart thumped in my chest. "Back? Back where?"

"Back to the oil rigs. North Sea. I live in Aberdeen," he explained. "I came down here to see…" There was a silence. "…to see Jim Pirie. He's an old friend of mine, so I lent a helping hand. I'll be back in the Spring. Around the end of March."

"I can wait," I said, looking into those dark, familiar eyes.

"No, you can't," Dan said tenderly. "Teenage boys can't wait. And they shouldn't wait. Go off and find somebody your own age."

"Do you mean you'll forget...?" I began to protest.

He put a finger against my lips. "Of course I won't forget. A boy like you comes along maybe once or twice in a lifetime. But I'm a man, you're a boy, and remember what the song says, 'Boys just wanna have fun.'"

I was about to correct him when I realised he was only teasing me. And I realised he was right. What had he told me? He liked boys, but he liked men and women, too. I was only fifteen. I had to give myself those chances.

Dan kissed me on the forehead, and suddenly I was only a kid. I extended my hand and shook his in what, I like to think, was a manly way. At that moment the door swung open and Mr Pirie walked in.

"Looks like I've arrived just in time." He surveyed the granary. "Looks like you two have done a first class job." My chest swelled with pride. "Well, Guy Tilson..."

"It's 'Tiger' Tilson," corrected Dan.

"Well, Tiger Tilson," said Mr Pirie without missing a beat, "looks like you've paid your debt to society. C'mon. It's getting dark already. I'll give you a lift back to the school." I nodded, then turned to Dan. I said, "Thanks, Dan, thanks for everything," and tried to say a whole lot more with my eyes.

"Thank you, Tiger," said Dan, "you sure made it a day to remember." I stepped out of the granary door and out of Dan's life.

We reached the school entrance. Mr Pirie dropped me off. "And, Tiger," he said, "remember to keep off the farm unless you let me know you're visiting. And you can visit any time." My smile must have lit up the dark.

"Thanks, sir, you're a sport. And, sir, could you give my best wishes to Dan again? He made it a great day."

"I'm not surprised," said Mr Pirie. "Dan Anthony's a good guy. I'll be sure to pass on the message." I was almost too stunned to ask the question that exploded inside my head.

Over the sound of the running engine, I said, "Mr Pirie, sir, there's a Jamie Anthony at our school. Has he got anything to do with Dan, Dan Anthony?"

The farmer cut the engine and called me over. He looked at me shrewdly. "You really are a bright young man, Guy Tilson. Dan's Jamie's father. Jamie's parents are divorced, messy business. Dan used to be in the fashion business; he's in oil now. He comes down a couple of times a year to keep an eye on Jamie." Mr Pirie gave me a serious look. "Jamie doesn't know. It's better that he doesn't. Can we count on you to keep our secret?"

I nodded. I was getting good at keeping secrets.

"Good night then, lad. Take care. Give my best wishes to Dr Honeyman when you see him. And if you're ever serious about being a farmer's boy, just let me know." He switched on, revved the engine and disappeared into the dusk.

I walked into school, a thousand thoughts fighting for my attention. I could feel Dan Anthony's cum squish around my arse hole. That cum had millions of sperm in it. A little sperm like that had helped create Jamie Anthony. Must have been a helluva good-looking sperm.

I burst out laughing.

To be a farmer's boy…

What a crazy world!

What a fucking crazy world!

Chapter 12

Next morning I felt like a shagged-out tomcat as I lay stretching myself under my duvet on a bright morning. My bumhole burned. The head of my cock felt as if it had been rubbed with sandpaper. Satisfying feelings both. I snuggled down for a long lie-in, which in our case meant until nine o'clock. No such luck.

I was drifting off, imagining my mouth round Dan's horsecock while my prick twitched up his hairy hole, anatomically impossible I know, but all things are possible in dreams.

"Get up! Get up! We're in trouble." I was shaken not stirred to a semblance of alertness. Tony Honeyman was sitting on the edge of my bed. He was white-faced. For a moment I feared he'd been caught in flagrante delicto, which you can loosely translate as his pants down, his prick up, possibly Michael Fletcher's bottom. No, he was the son of the Headmaster and proprietor. It had to be something worse than that.

I rolled onto my back and opened my eyes. My morning erection tented the duvet. Tony gave it a cheerful smack.

"It's Tim. He's down with glandular fever," Tony blurted. Tony never 'blurted'; this was serious. "He's in the San., but he's going home this afternoon. He won't be back till the new term. We're screwed."

"Shafted!"

"Buggered!"

Tony sat on the bed absent-mindedly squeezing my bulge while we put our collective mind to the problem. I pushed his hand away. I can't think with an erection. Or rather, a hard-on does my thinking for me.

"Let's have breakfast," I said. "Then let's meet in the Music

Room and plan things from there. I'll call Peter. Get a couple of juniors to set our stuff up. We may need to revise our programme."

"If we're able to do the Festival at all," muttered Tony gloomily.

Half an hour later, the five of us were in the Music Room. Five because Tony had recruited Michael Fletcher and Jamie Anthony to set up the equipment. I was a little embarrassed to find Jamie there; some of his father's sperm were probably swimming blindly in my bowels looking for an egg to fertilise. The only egg in me was boiled, and it wasn't in my bowels, not yet any way. Just looking at Jamie reminded me of Dan. I ignored an incipient hard-on.

We tried a couple of the numbers with just two guitars, Peter and myself, and Tony on the drums. The sound was decidedly thin. Then we got to 'Get It On' by T. Rex which we'd only been doing as a sort of leg-pull since the idea of Peter 'getting it on' was remote in the extreme. I've seen a sexier stick insect in the biology cages. Guitar work: 10, Voice: 10, Sex Quotient: nul points! We were pretty dejected when Jamie piped up.

"Hey, that's the song Mike and me are doing in the Talent Show."

I resisted correcting his grammar. "What are you talking about?"

"'Get It On', the Marc Bolan track," piped Jamie. "We've got T. Rex backing tracks. We're also going to do 'Summertime Blues' and even 'Teenage Dream'…" Mike finished his sentence, "…If they don't throw you off the stage first." I understood what they meant. The Christmas Talent Show could be a pretty violent affair. Acts that didn't come off, especially junior acts, were regularly fed to the lions by a boozed up Sixth Form. By tradition, no masters attended the Talent Show.

Peter took up the idea. "I must say the idea's appealing. T. Rex were big in Brazil when we were there. I know the chords for most of their numbers, the lyrics, too." Tony gave him a look of absolute contempt but it was tinged with a kind of desperate hope. "Go on then, show us what you can do."

Peter launched into the opening riff of 'Get It On', then pulled back to show me the basic chords. Tony found the beat, the tempo and the rhythm with ease; it was hardly the most complicated of songs. It took us about twenty minutes to have the semblance of a performance in place; we just didn't have the voices.

I rigged up an extra mike, did the 'Hello, Mike,' joke, and planted the junior boys in front of it. Peter hit the opening riff, Tony brought in the beat, I added the bass, and Peter, Michael and Jamie launched into the song. The effect was electric. It sounded like Michael Jackson, backed by the Supremes, impersonating Marc Bolan and T. Rex. While Pete stood almost stock still, the younger boys gyrated, pouted and posed at the mike, swinging their hips and thrusting their crotches in a bump and grind routine that would have impressed a pro. 'Dirty sweet' wasn't in it! This was sheer filth. I had a raging hard-on long before we hit the chorus.

We gasped to the end of the song as if we were having a collective orgasm. Utter silence, apart from heavy breathing, as the final guitar notes died away. Jamie turned to me. He tossed back that dark glossy hair and asked in all innocence, "Do you think they'll let us do a second song?"

"Not with your trousers on," I said. I laughed and turned to Tony. It's not often one saw Honeyman stunned. He pulled himself together. "Fletcher, Anthony, welcome to The Ram Stam Boys." The boys whooped and punched the air. "Now let's try the others."

"Just one thing," I said. "If they're part of Ram Stam, it's Mike and Jamie. That's Pete. I'm Guy. And you're Tony." I'm not sure where the courage to say that came from. A thought flickered across Tony's face, "Right on. Now let's get it on. Let's try 'Summertime Blues'. Pete, lead the way."

The next two hours were brilliant. We sang as if we'd been rehearsing for weeks. Sometimes the sound was dangerously near the Spice Girls but Pete was always able to make his guitar just that bit raunchier. We had to tone down the boys now and again; after all, we weren't sure just who the jury would be and how much they could take. We also had to stop them switching the line to "You're dirty sweet and you're my boy!"

In the afternoon Tony arrived at our second rehearsal with great news. Dr Honeyman had okayed the inclusion of Mike and Jamie on three conditions: one, Adrian Ackerley would come along; two, Allan Litchfield, the school caretaker, would drive the minibus; three, we'd have to stay overnight in a hotel in Cambridge, the last because he didn't want Allan driving us back after midnight. It would be brilliant to have Ackerley along. And Allan hated pop music so much he'd spend the entire competition in the nearest bar, then collapse in his hotel room, leaving us entirely to our own (de)vices!

The next eight days were spent in a frenzy of rehearsal. We added '20th Century Boy' to our repertoire just in case we won and had to do an encore.

We decided to forego any dressing up. Trainers, old jeans, and cut off T-shirts would do. When Dr Honeyman came along to one rehearsal, however, we wore toned-down versions of the school uniform, and toned down our performance till it looked like a rehearsal for the Christmas Carol Service at our local church.

Chapter 13

On the last Saturday morning before we broke up for Christmas, The Ram Stam Boys bussed out of school, cheered by a hundred boys giving us the V for victory salute. Well, that's what I interpreted it as. The drive took forty minutes, and we reached our hotel near Market Square by ten o'clock.

We piled into the hotel with a hold-all each and were shown our rooms. Luckily enough, we were all on the top floor while Allan was on the first floor. We had three double rooms: Tony and Adrian, Mike and Jamie, Pete and myself. We quickly changed into jeans, shirts and trainers, located Allan in the bar, and bussed our way to Market Hall. The place was already crammed with boys and girls from a dozen schools, state and public, most of them shepherded by bewildered teachers who, like Allan, wanted to be elsewhere. Unlike them, Allan already was elsewhere.

We were given make-shift changing rooms at the rear of the hall, but warned there was no space for rehearsal. We were given the running order. Our luck was out. Ram Stam were on last of the fifteen performances. The audience would surely have had enough by then. Our luck was in. Judging was to be done not by teachers but by 'Audience Acclimation' and 'The Magic of the Clapometer'. That's exactly what it said. At least we wouldn't be performing until just after three. We could sit in the audience, relax, loosen up and get rid of those butterflies. We'd also be having lunch and Allan, gourmet that he was, had booked places at McDonald's. We might not win, but we would have fun.

The first act was a spotty girl with specs playing a harp, followed by a boy with an oversize cello between his legs. He looked like he was being violated by a particularly clumsy monster. The third act was a violent duet; yes, a 'violent' duet;

it was played on violins, but the boy and girl involved attacked their instruments as if they truly hated them. Saw, saw, buzz, buzz. The audience were growing restless; paper aeroplanes flew here and there, boys developed hacking coughs, peanuts rained down from the balcony. If this went on, it was likely we'd never get on stage.

The fourth act turned the tide and demonstrated that Ram Stam would have serious competition. A black boy about my age, wearing tails and bow tie, walked onto the stage and bowed to the audience. There was a storm of catcalls, none of which had to do with colour, all of which had to do with the prospect of more classical music. He sat down before a Steiner piano. Hands raised, fingers poised, he hit those keys like Jerry Lee Lewis himself. This was rock 'n roll with balls on. The good-looking bastard hammered his way through three rock numbers, each one ending in a storm of applause. For the first time, the Clapometer bucked into real life, shooting up to 97 out of a possible 100. If that kid had been able to sing to his playing, it would have been all over for The Ram Stam Boys. I thought about being coloured. That was being different, too, but at least you weren't faced with the prospect of having one day to come out of the closet and tell your mother.

Acts came and went; some good, some bad, some downright awful. One group playing Stones' numbers got 86, but the audience weren't happy about 'old foggeys' stuff. I only hoped that most of the audience would think our T. Rex numbers were original. And I hoped the macho set wouldn't be put off by two pretty boys thrusting cocks at them while singing like the Spice Girls. We'd have the girls and the gays in the audience, and the paedophiles and pederasts among the teachers, but adults didn't have a vote, so fuck them.

It was quiet over lunch. I'd never seen big Macs eaten with so much dignity before. Allan didn't show up. Ackerley was in charge and he was gently supportive. He'd seen our act a couple of times. "I can't pretend I enjoy contemporary pop music," he said, "but I have to admit the sound you lot make is hard to get out of one's head. I even find myself tapping my foot."

"You'll be slapping your knees next if you're not careful," growled Tony. Everybody laughed and relaxed. We shared the bonus of Allan's Big Mac.

Back at Market Hall, we watched the acts until around three o'clock when we were summoned to the 'rehearsal rooms'. "Get your equipment ready, boy," an organiser explained. "When that curtain closes on Number 14, you've got three minutes to get set up. Then the curtain opens and away you go. Good luck." As we pulled off our sweaters and revealed the cutaway shirts, the chap blinked and whistled. "Far out, boys, fucking far out. What are you called?" He glanced at the programme. "The Ram Stam Boys! Too fucking true." We gave him a collective grin; we'd made one fan at least.

The sound of Number 14's trombone died away. The curtains swished. Ackerley took charge. We were set up within two minutes. Tony looked around and, in a stage whisper, said, "Right, Ram Stam, let's show them what we've got."

The audience didn't cheer, it exploded. And then for the first few moments they sat in silence. Pete hit the opening chords, Tony thumped in with the drums, I slung bass notes under the whole thing. Pete, huskier than I'd ever heard him, "Well, you're dirty 'n sweet…" I don't think the audience understood a fucking word, but that didn't matter, they got the message. And when Jamie and Mike reached "Get it on, bang the gong," they went fucking berserk.

Carried away, Jamie and Mike swung into a bump-and-grind routine that would have had them arrested in a public place. Only when the curtains closed did we discover that

Jamie's fly was wide open, his zip glinting under the spotlight. For a minute, I thought Pete would freeze, but it was exactly the opposite. We went straight into 'Summertime Blues' and he began to sway at the hips as if his legs were going to give way. His voice took on a slight warble that made him sound as if he had the hiccups. The effect was startling. I shot a quizzical look at Tony who gave me a drum roll that shook the stage. My bass notes turned into a slow fucking rhythm as if a hot, hard cock was being driven up my arse.

As 'Summertime Blues' died away, we hammered straight into '20th Century Boy' which was exactly the way to finish the show. Kids were up on their seats, rocking in the aisles, clapping above their heads, and screwing in the balcony (as far as we knew). It was exhilarating but scary at the same time.

We reached the end, the very end. The hall was bedlam. The arrow on the Clapometer shot up and stuck on 100! The curtains swung close. Sweat poured from all of us. The organiser came over.

"We can do an encore if you like," panted Tony. "We'll do 'London Boys'."

"You bloody well will not," the guy yelled above the din. I began to suspect he was not a teacher. "Get your stuff and get your sweet little asses out of this place. Use the Fire Doors over there. And you…" He pointed at Jamie. "Pull your zip up. We want to keep our licence. They'll send your prizes on to you."

As we dragged our stuff out the back door, the guy called again. "Hey, what hotel are you lot staying at. I'd like to bring over your prizes myself." I looked at him. He was grinning and squeezing his crotch. I grinned back and gripped my own. "Go fuck yourself," I shouted. "Looks like I'll have to," he shouted back.

We hid round the back of the Hall. Fortunately, Adrian

had a spare set of keys to the minibus. He couldn't drive it but we bundled our stuff in, locked the doors and went to find Allan. We found him at the fifth attempt in the 'Hounds & Hares'. He was far from drunk but he was decidedly cheerful. We left the bus where it was and made our way back to the hotel.

In a state of high excitement we explained to Allan how we'd won. "Right, then," he said gruffly, as if we'd announced we all had mumps, "we'd better celebrate. You've got a couple of hours to calm down, clean up and rest up. Be ready at eight. We're going out for a slap-up meal, and it's all on the Mortician," he glanced at Tony. "That's Dad to you, and Dr Honeyman to the rest of you. Now bugger off, leave me in peace, and for God's sake, have a shower. You stink like old beaver."

We raced straight into the lounge, ordered Cokes all round, and spent the next hour going over our entire performance, note by note, line by line. We still couldn't believe the audience had reacted like that. We were good, but not that good, were we? Finally, we realised how exhausted we were and made for our rooms where the bathrooms were en suite. We agreed to meet in the lounge at 7.45 on the dot; nobody to be late for any reason.

Peter showered first. He came out of the bathroom with a large white and blue-striped towel wrapped round his middle. I dumped my clothes where I stood and, respecting his modesty, slipped quickly away. It was bliss to stand under the hot showers, caressing my body with soap and reliving those magical minutes on stage. Finding I was getting an erection, I spent the last few minutes under cold water to cool my ardour. It would be hard enough sleeping alone in a room with Peter Parker without giving into temptation this soon.

I returned to the bedroom, a towel wrapped round my middle. I was pleasantly surprised to find Pete stretched out his bed, his towel draped across his middle. I'd half expected him to be in some kind of chastity belt. I stood at the end of my bed and toweled myself dry, demonstrating that I didn't give a fig about nudity, his or mine. As I dried my hair, I felt my semi-tumescent penis bounce between my thighs. Ah well, I'd never claimed I was a saint.

Peter was right. It was too warm to put on clothes. I bounced onto my bed and bunched my towel modestly over my groin.

"Great, isn't it?" I said.

"What is?"

"Everything. The festival. The competition. The Ram Stam Boys. Being away from school. Being here with you." The last remark slipped out but I was beyond caring. I let out a deep sigh of contentment. If Peter didn't know how I felt about him by now, he never would.

"What do you think the others are doing?"

"Probably having sex." The silence was as humid as the bathroom. "Look, Pete, you're no fool. You know that some of us have sex with each other. That's the way it is. It doesn't mean that much. Maybe some of us are gay, maybe not. Who the Hell cares? As long as I'm not harming anyone, I'm going to do what I jolly well please. Actually, if you weren't here, I'd probably be lying back, playing with myself, dreaming about…" I left the thought dangling in the space between us. Peter's response was totally unexpected.

"I'm scared," he said, in a voice so low I wasn't sure I'd heard properly. "I've never told anyone about it."

I didn't understand what he meant. "Tell me," I said. "You know all about me, but you still like me. Maybe that's what makes true friends."

I got off my bed and moved over to his. For a moment I stood there. Then Pete edged over to make room for me. We lay side by side. Pete looked into the distance and began.

"I was about nine years old," he said. "We were in Brazil. My family had a station, a missionary station in a logging town up the Amazon. We were ministering to the Indians." Images of a semi-naked Charlie Boorman in 'Emerald Forest' danced in my mind. "I was taking after-school piano lessons from Mrs. Murray and Mom had to pick me up every day. One day, she was busy with something at work, so she called a taxicab to pick me up and bring me home. Mrs. Murray walked me to the cab and instructed the driver. She was a bit concerned because the driver seemed so young.

"The cab driver was of mixed race, bit of Portuguese and Indian. He was good-looking, even at nine I knew that. He smiled at me and invited me to sit up front with him so we'd both have company. I waved good-bye to Mrs. Murray and hopped right in.

"The driver, Pedro, started talking to me, saying how cute I looked in my whites, T-shirt, shorts, socks and sunhat. He asked me how old I was. He said that pretty soon I'd be turning into a man. Did I know what happened then? I shook my head. I listened, wide-eyed. This was a topic my mother and father had never broached. He said there were lots of differences between men and boys. It was important to know about them. He could show me if I wanted."

Peter turned to me with eyes pleading for understanding. "I really didn't know what he meant. Honest, Guy, I didn't."

I tousled his damp hair. "Of course you didn't, Pete. You were only a kid." He smiled at me and relaxed as he resumed the story.

"We were winding through a dense bit of jungle. It was almost a dirt road. Pedro pulled off to one side and cut the engine. We were surrounding by thick foliage. It was as cool and as quiet as it ever gets in the jungle. He pushed the seats way back and turned to face me. He was talking a lot and saying that men and boys were different in lots of ways, but that there was one way that was most important. Then he unzipped his pants and pulled out his thing!

"I was really scared," Peter shivered. "I just knew Mom and Dad wouldn't think it was right for me to be looking at that, so I shut my eyes. Pedro kept on talking, saying that not very many boys got such a good chance to see how a man was made. He started explaining what it was for, but that sounded so gross I blanked most of it out. My eyes were still closed, but my curiosity was bigger than my fright, so I opened my eyes a little bit to see what was going on.

"Pedro's thing was sticking straight up in the air, like a stick of rock coming right out of his pants. He was touching it all over, trailing his fingers up and down and all around, especially on the end. He was looking at me, his smile bigger than ever. He asked me if I liked to look at his 'dick' and I said 'I guess so,' but just so I wouldn't make him mad.

"Pedro told me to look closely at his 'dick' and notice how big and strong it was. Despite myself, I looked down to see that his thing had got even bigger, and the end was now all swollen and purple. It looked kinda gross and scary, but fascinating, too. He took his hand off it for a moment, spit into his hand, and smeared the spit all over himself. I remember thinking to myself that it was nearly as long as the ruler in my schoolbox. I could see it was jumping around between his fingers.

"Next he wanted me to show him something. He said he wouldn't touch me, but seeing my thing would help him get rid of his stiffness. I remember wondering at first if he was talking about somebody's pet, but he pointed at my penis. He said if I pulled the legs of my shorts and underpants over to one side, he could tell me what colour hair I'd have down there when I was eleven or twelve.

"I can't remember all the feelings I was going through. Part of me was intensely curious, part of me just wanted to get home. And part of me was making my penis stiffen in my underpants. I had to do something.

"Anyway, I reached down and pulled the thin cotton fabrics over to one side and my dick jumped out. It was really embarrassing because it had gone stiff. It was only a couple of inches long but it looked hot and angry. When I looked back over at him, I saw his hand was moving real fast as he pumped his fist up and down his own greasy pole. He was staring at my dick like it was the most interesting object in the world. Then with his spare hand, he reached over and using two fingers and his thumb he began to masturbate me. I didn't know that's what it was at the time. All I knew was what Pedro was doing was thrilling and terrifying at the same time. I could actually feel my penis harden and lengthen under his fingers as if it had a mind of its own.

"When he saw I was looking hard at his thing, he began to talk real fast about what a great little kid I was. Showing him my 'little cock' while he 'jacked off his big old dick' for me. I looked up and was rather scared how red his face had got. His eyes were shining as he looked between my legs. As I watched, he gave a big groan, shut his eyes, and told me to watch him 'shoot his load', whatever that meant.

"Suddenly, Pedro lifted his bottom off the seat and made a groaning sound. Gobs of white stuff started to squirt out of the end of his dick. It looked like the paste glue we used to make in kindergarten. The first spurts shot way into the air, the rest squished out in little pumping waves. There was a real mess on the steering wheel, the dashboard and even the window. His fingers were still working on my erection, and my bottom had started to squirm on the seat. Something terrible, something wonderful was happening down there.

"Without any warning, he leaned over me and swallowed my little prick. I was terrified. I thought he was going to bite it off. I was the son of missionaries, so I knew what cannibals did to us. I tried to push his head away, but he was too strong. The sucking was hot and wet. It seemed to draw me right out of my own body. It was my bottom lifting off the seat at this time. Then I felt myself explode, no, not explode, fragment is a better word. I was splitting up into a million pieces. I was totally embarrassed, too, because I was pushing my dick deeper into the man's mouth and loving it.

"I felt like I'd fainted. I fell back on the seat and closed my eyes. I felt his fingers tucking my penis back under my pants and shorts. The engine started up again and we were back on the road. Pedro told me I couldn't ever tell anybody about what he showed me, because little kids aren't supposed to learn about this until later. He said I could trust him. He wouldn't tell anybody about our secret. And he said if I needed a taxi again, I should ask for Pedro, if I wanted to learn more secrets.

"When he dropped me off at home, I ran up to my room and threw myself onto my bed. I was in turmoil. I wanted to tell my mother what had happened, but I couldn't because… because I'd liked it so much. I pulled down my shorts and pants. My penis was a bit red but otherwise it looked okay. I did what Pedro had done with my own fingers. I started to stiffen. The good feeling started to come back. I was thrilled and terrified. I pulled up my things, went downstairs and played the piano for two hours. I never told anyone anything until now."

I turned to Peter and turned his face to me. He looked solemn but in a way more relaxed than I'd seen him before.

"It wasn't your fault, Pete," I said. "You were only nine years old."

"I know that," he whispered, "but I enjoyed it, I enjoyed that man touching me."

"Of course you did," I said. "There's nothing wrong with that. Having your penis touched by someone else is an enjoyable experience. What he did was wrong; not what you did. Because you were too young to decide for yourself. He took advantage of you. It was all one-sided. Everybody has to be free to make up their own mind. You weren't old enough to do that. He did it for you, and that's wrong."

Suddenly grinning at me, Peter said, "But now that I'm safe with you, I want to rub your dick until you squirt your stuff while you play with my itchy hole." I was flabbergasted. Where had this new Peter Parker come from?

He hugged me. "Remember the day I found you and Mike in your bedroom. I told you I had a lot to learn about my new school. Well, I've been watching and learning. I think I'm ready for my first practical lesson."

My erection tented my bath towel at ninety degrees. For some reason, the idea of little Pete Parker getting his first sex lesson in a taxicab somewhere up the Amazon had pulled my trigger. My cock was as hard as a crowbar. It was a relief to chuck away the towel. Peter did the same. As I suspected, he was beautiful. Not quite as long as me but certainly thicker. He stuck up pink and proud from a forest of dark curly hair. His balls seemed huge; understandable when you think of the juice he must have built up in them.

He twisted his bum around until we were both comfortable. "Can I touch you?" he asked, a slight tremble in his voice.

"OK, but you have to do what I tell you to do. This will be an educational experience for you." Peter rolled his eyes and explained his father was always labeling things he didn't want to do 'educational experiences.' At last here was one he could really enjoy. As he reached for my cock, I noticed a fine film of sweat on his upper lip.

"You've got to be gentle at first," I said. "You know you can hurt a guy if you grab his dick too hard. Even more so with his balls. Hold me just like you hold yourself." I saw

Peter's face redden. "Pete," I asked, "you do toss yourself off now and again, don't you?"

"Not really," he said, "Touching yourself is a sin. Tossing yourself off sends you to Hell."

I'm afraid I laughed. "Maybe, but not right away, so let's have fun first. Then, see you in Hell!" Thank God, or whoever organises these things, Pete laughed.

He moved his hand almost reverently to my throbbing meat. His fingers wrapped around the pulsing muscle and gave it a gentle squeeze. "Oooo," he said, "it's so soft and hard and hot, all at the same time!" He lowered his face to have a closer inspection. I twisted further round so that we were almost in a sixty-nine position.

Leaving Peter to explore my dick, I leaned over to inspect his bumhole. I was particularly interested to learn if my middle finger would fit inside his rosy pucker. I gently nudged his legs wider. He needed no further hint: his legs spread wide open at my touch. The contrast of the smooth, powdery, hairless anal lips set in darker skin looked good enough to eat. Nothing ventured, nothing gained, I gave his ring a tentative slurp. I felt Pete's fingers tighten round my swollen cock.

As his hand began to move up and down on my cock, I moved my hand underneath his balls and into his darker meat. With my middle finger, I searched out his little pink rose. As the boy realized what I was doing, he spread his legs wider and started to pump my penis with his whole hand. My finger found its target. Carefully, I inserted it to the first knack. The hot shower had helped him loosen up considerably. I heard him whisper huskily above me.

"Oh, Guy!" he cried. "That feels wonderful! Your finger is so fat it's filling me up... Your dick is starting to leak some stuff on my hand!" Naturally, he didn't have to tell me that, because I could feel that I was going to be cumming pretty quick.

His naked little shithole gripped my finger tightly, I began to jiggle it in and out to loosen him up as much as possible. I could tell he appreciated the new sensation by the enthusiasm he was giving my cock. Pete hadn't seen cum since he was nine years old; he was going to make up for that pretty soon!

Suddenly I felt my cock swell. "I'm cumming," I called out, sliding my finger in and out of his asshole quite ruthlessly. I could feel the sperm race along my urethra. Then I felt something hot and wet close over the top half of my cock. I was pumping into Peter's mouth. That made me cum twice as hard, and I felt jet after jet spurt into his mouth. Lionhearted Christian that he was, Peter sank his mouth even deeper over me until I felt his lips brush my pubic hair. God, for a novice, this boy was good!

As the last few drops squeezed out of me, I withdrew my finger and slid up Pete's body. His eyes were glazed, his lips puffy and swollen, dribbles of cum at each side of his mouth. Even his nipples looked erect. I kissed away my own cum. "Why did you do that?" I asked. "Do what?" "Swallow my cum?" "Because I remembered the mess Pedro made. This is a hotel. We shouldn't mess up their sheets. And besides…" He coughed and grinned. "…it just seemed the right thing to do."

I kissed him again and started the long slide down his body. He took me by the hair and pulled me back up. I gave him my questioning look.

"We've got all night," he said. "There's only half an hour before we meet the others. Could you just hold me for a bit?" We cuddled into each other. "And do you mind if I kiss you?" he whispered. My answer was to kiss him full on the lips, the tip of my tongue searching for entry. He opened wide to take me in.

At last it was happening.
I was not only having sex, I was making love.

Chapter 14

Forty five minutes later we were ensconced in plush seats in Garfinkels, arguing the toss over the menu. Allan had had a quiet word with the manager, then left us secure in the knowledge he was ensconced in the 'Fog & Fuck' two doors away. Although glasses were put on our table, no Cokes were forthcoming. We understood why when the manager brought a huge pitcher of lager, "Courtesy of your manager. And, of course, only the older boys may partake." He didn't wink; he didn't have to.

I settled for grilled mushrooms for starters, followed by steak and chips with a black pepper sauce, followed by a ginormous slice of Black Forest Gateau. The festival and the sex had given me a real appetite but I didn't over-indulge. The thought of what I might be 'eating' later that evening kept me sensible. Not so Jamie and Michael, who got sillier and sillier as the evening progressed, thanks to the lager and their own high spirits. But their silliness was genuinely funny, and we were all in the mood to forgive everything.

Tony and Adrian drank around five pints each, but they remained reasonably sober, possibly because they embarked on a serious discussion about how far Ram Stam could go. What had happened in that hall had been phenomenal. Boys bands were still big business, but here was one that could actually play, and had two young lads prettier than anything in Hanson.

I followed the conversation as well as I could, but I was distracted by the colour of Peter's eyes, the way his hair brushed his collar, the tilt of his nose, the shape of his fingers, and the way his grin was slightly lop-sided. Several times I wanted to brush his cheek. I may have done it a couple of times as the lager took hold; either nobody noticed or nobody cared. It was that kind of night.

Around 10.30, Tony signaled that the meal was over. Apparently everything had been taken care of. The bill had been paid. We were to walk the few blocks to our hotel. Allan wanted everybody up by eight in the morning. We strolled back to the hotel singing T. Rex numbers. It was a cold, clear night with a million stars overhead. I looked up and thought of Jamie. He was dancing on ahead with Michael. Tony and Adrian brought up the rear, still in earnest conversation. Peter and I strolled contentedly along. The walk was all too short, so Adrian led us by another route that skirted some of the university buildings. We were still so high we could have walked for hours. But at 11.30 we found ourselves in the hotel lift heading for the top floor. Our great day was nearly over; the night wasn't. We did a final chorus of 'Get It On' and ran for our rooms before the management arrived.

In our room I was taken aback when Peter took over. He threw his jacket and sweater on an armchair. Then he took off mine. "Give me a hand," he said, and proceeded to push his bed alongside mine. "C'mere," he said. Meekly, a bit unsteadily, I obeyed.

He undid my shirt and slid it from my shoulders. He pushed me back on the bed. He knelt and undid my shoes and pulled them off. My socks followed. "Stand up." Still kneeling, he undid my belt, unzipped me and drew down my trousers and underpants. He circled my stomach with his wet lips again and again. He kissed my belly button. He licked my pubic hair until it was sopping wet. All the while he squeezed the cheeks of my bottom.

My cock sprang up and hit him in the face. With one hand he jacked me gently as his lips slipped over the head of my cock. He pulled the foreskin back. He ran the head around the inside of his mouth. He took it out and stuck the tip of his tongue in the little slit. The cock was running with sweat, pre-cum glazed the head and the upper shaft. With his free hand he squeezed my balls gently. Just when I felt the sap rising, he pushed me back onto the bed. I moved so that I was sitting with my back against a headboard, watching him. I don't think he meant to do a strip-tease but that's what it looked like.

Peter switched on the bed lamps, walked to the door and flicked off the main light. Standing in the middle of the room, he disrobed slowly. As he pushed down his trousers and socks, he turned away. His tight little bum stuck high in the air. He held the position while he undid and slid off his shoes and socks. Then he amazed me by pulling his bumcheeks wide apart. By the glow of the lamps, I saw his little puckered virgin centre. That was what he was offering me. I kept my hands away from my cock. I knew if I touched myself I would fountain immediately. Peter came over and lay alongside me on the bed, his head resting on the board. He turned, kissed me and whispered.

"You'll have to show me what to do."

"Are you sure?" I asked.

"Absolutely."

I slid down the bed till I was kneeling between his legs. I pulled them and Peter slid flat on his back. "Pass me a pillow." I slid the pillow under the small of his back, raising his bum. "Open your legs." He opened them wide. I nuzzled in and parted his cheeks with my hands, my thumbs opening him wide. I dove in face-first and ran my tongue around his anal ring. I could swear I felt it twitch.

"Hold yourself open," I instructed him. With Peter holding his buttocks apart, it was much easier. I licked and licked the length of his ring, a free hand grasping his cock and working it gently. He was as stiff and hard as milk bottle. As I pushed past his ring with the tip of my tongue, he moaned.

"Oh, shit, that's good." I raised my head up and grinned.

"Oh, good, I hope that's not shit!" I said, not caring one jot what I'd find up his canal as long as there was room for my prick. After a few minutes, over half my tongue was up his bum. Two fingers joined my tongue, at least inside the rim as I worked and relaxed his sphincter muscle. After ten minutes, he was loose enough for me to withdraw my tongue and slide in two, then three fingers. Fortunately his sweat and my spit made the greasy passage not too difficult but I know I was hurting him.

The moment of truth arrived. I lifted each leg and draped it over a shoulder, mine, then worked my kneeling body deeper between Peter's legs until my cock was well wedged in his crack. I hauled at him until he slid down the bed and raised his legs almost vertical. We were able to look at each other. He smiled, maybe grimaced a little, and I leaned over to kiss him on the mouth. I slid one hand round to jerk his cock; that would distract him from the pain without detracting from the pleasure. His assorted grunts and moans told me he was experiencing a blend of both.

The head of my cock found his hot greasy hole. I pushed. He winced. I pushed again. "Relax," I whispered. "Don't fight it, just let it happen." He nodded, droplets of sweat falling from his face onto his chest. His eyes were wide and wild. I pushed harder. There might have been a plop. I was in! The head of my cock plugged up his arse. Carefully, I transferred my weight to my hips and felt myself slide in deeper. I make up in length what I miss in thickness, and that helped. Suddenly without effort, I was sliding in all the way.

I began to jerk my hips, letting each forward jerk push me in, each backward jerk draw me out. My dick felt like it was in a hot, spongy treacle pudding. I could feel my balls brush tightly in his crack. His ring gripped me like an elastic collar; the friction was wonderful. I looked up at Peter. His eyes were closed now. There was a smile on his lips. Sometimes he'd wince, but pleasure had over-taken pain. He was being butt-fucked and loving it; I was doing the butt-fucking and loving every inch of it.

I'm not sure I heard the bedroom door open and close. Suddenly Jamie and Mike were there. One perched on either side of the bed. For a moment panic set in. I looked at Peter. His eyes flickered open, then closed again. He was too far gone to care. I glanced back at the boys. Their pyjamas were off. They were in the nude. They were giggling.

Something wriggled between my body as it arched and fell. It was Michael's head. He kept it on Peter's stomach but slid down to take in the top three inches of Peter's prick. As I rose, Mike slid further down Pete's erection, sucking hard; as I stroked my prick in deep, Mike's head slid further up Pete's body. Pete was groaning openly now; his head rolling from side to side, saliva dribbling from his mouth. "This must be as good as it gets," I thought. I was wrong. It got better.

Fingers slid round the base of my prick. Each time I withdrew they jerked me rapidly and fiercely. A small hand pried open my buttocks, a small face dove in. It was Jamie. He was licking my butt hole, pressing the tip of his hot little tongue until my sphincter opened to receive him. It was hard to take in; not his tongue, but what was happening.

Pete was being fucked and sucked at the same time. I was fucking Pete while Jamie jerked me off and sucked my anus. Michael was sucking Pete. I had a feeling that when this was over, there were going to be two juniors desperately in need of sucking if not fucking. And this was going to be over soon.

My hips took over control and started to ram my prick in deep again and again without respite. I felt my cock swell inside Pete's rectum. Images spun in my head out of control as the sperm raged in my balls. I felt Pete toss and turn on the bed—"like a virgin, fucked for the very first time".

Once it started, I couldn't get the fucking tune out of my

head. Then I realised it was Jamie Anthony. He was humming the tune as he sawed two, three, surely not four fingers in and out of my butt. This time the shooting stars went off in my brain. They went off right up Pete's arse. I heard gurgling and realised Mike's head was trapped between us as Pete shot his own load into the boy's mouth. "Serves him fucking right," I thought before a tinge of panic set in.

Whatever Ram Stam meant, it was happening on that 'double bed' in a Cambridge hotel room. Four boys fucking, sucking and having fun. I might have blacked out, I don't know. I know the four of us ended up in each other's arms, sprawled amongst our own tangled legs and arms, sweat streaming as we adjusted our positions, semen between Pete's legs and on Michael's lips.

The kids were giggling. It didn't seem strange that I thought of Jamie and Michael as kids. They were demanding to know when it was their turn. "Suck me," said Jamie. "Suck me," said Michael. "Fuck both of you," said I. "Yes, please," they chorused together.

But it was no good. I was so tired that all I wanted to do was fall asleep in Peter's arms. That was no good. He was already sound asleep in mine.

"Can we stay here tonight?" That was Michael.

"We're going to. We've brought our duvets." That was Jamie.

As I fell asleep, I realised they were still on the bed, but they'd changed positions. Jamie and Mike were lying head to toe, pleasuring each other with their mouths and fingers. The quiet sucking and slurping was incredibly soothing, incredibly right.

The door burst open at 7 in the morning. I knew it was 7 because my digital watch went off at the precise moment Ackerley and Honeyman landed on our bed. There were squeals and howls of protest as Adrian and Tony burrowed their way under our duvets. Jamie's eyes looked up from the bottom of the bed like a disturbed lemur. He wriggled his way up to join us.

There we lay, half asleep: Peter, Jamie, Michael and myself, sprawled across the beds, each other and our dawn visitors who'd squeezed in what little space there was. At least they'd had the grace to close the door behind them.

Tony flicked on a bedside lamp, urging Adrian at the same time to, "Read it, go on, read that good bit." I shielded my eyes. Ackerley was holding a book, a huge paperback with a yellow and red cover. I assumed this would be something to do with The Ram Stam Boys. I forced open my sleep-glued eyes. Peter was wide awake. Jamie and Mike were snogging—dirty little beasts. I gave them a slap each.

"Go on, read that good bit, the bit about Shane," repeated Tony.

Shane! Who the fuck was Shane? I remembered the cowboy film. Who was the guy who played Shane? Alan somebody or other. Good-looking guy. But surely Ackerley wasn't going to read extracts from the novel 'Shane' at 7 in the morning, or at any time of the morning, come to think of it.

"'Shane has been my lasting sex partner for about six years,'" began Ackerley. "'When we have sex it usually happens like this: we watch television upstairs in my bedroom. Every now and then I glance at his crotch and imagine his cock. Then I start rubbing and caressing him there until he starts to respond. When it is time to go to bed we both get undressed and climb into bed. We then lie on top of each other and I start to caress his ass.'"

What the hell was this? I couldn't remember a scene like this in the movie?

"It's a boy talking about another boy," Ackerley interrupted himself. "This is true stuff. Want me to go on?" Nodding all round. Hands had already disappeared under the duvets.

"'He starts kissing me, a French kiss, and we do this for a few minutes,'" continued our benefactor. "'Then he moves down and starts sucking my nipples. Then he'll start licking my chest, my neck, and around my cock. Finally he takes my cock into his mouth and sucks on it until I come. He will then suck my balls and lick between my legs. Then he will lie on his back and let me go down on him.'"

The moles under the duvets were getting frantic. I gripped Peter's wrist. I wanted to cum, but not too quickly.

"'I start off by kissing him, then sucking his tits, his small but tasty cock, swallow what little preseminal fluid he has, suck his balls, lick in between his legs, and lick his asshole…. I definitely would love to be penetrated rectally by a dick. Shane already penetrates me with his finger and it feels very good, him moving his finger back and forth inside my asshole.'"

Jamie's head disappeared under a duvet. My hand followed him and dragged his head back into the light. He shrugged and grinned.

"What book is that?" asked Peter, breathing deeply before he spoke. Ackerley turned the book in our direction. "'The Sheer Shite Report'," I read aloud.

"It actually says 'The Shere Hite Report'," laughed Peter. "You're bit more short-sighted than you said. Ouch! That hurt!"

"It was meant to," I said, relaxing my grip on his erection.

"Shere Hite is American," explained Ackerley. "She does sex surveys, interviews mostly, then writes them up. I've read a couple of her books before. This one's about sex in the family."

"Whose family?" piped up Fletcher.

"Anybody's family. Lots of families," said Ackerley. "And I found this book…"

"We found it," interrupted Tony. "Yesterday. In the market. I bought it. It's mine."

"Read some more," said Jamie.

"'When did I have my best sex?'"

"With me," said Tony.

"Not while I'm reading," said Ackerley.

"'When my cousin came over to spend the night and we went up to my bedroom and locked the door. He started talking about sex with boys and what to do, how to do it. I was only thirteen and he was seventeen. We were on the bed and he took out his cock; it was huge, it was about three inches longer than mine. He started masturbating, his dick was really hard, and all of a sudden this white stuff came out.

"'We decided to go to bed, he told me to put my cock into his asshole, so I put it in, it felt so good. He took it out and he said roll over on your stomach and then he slid it in and he went up and down and he came and it felt good.'"

"Great," sighed Jamie. He threw back the duvet. He and Michael were naked and erect, a hand wrapped around each other's cock, jacking it gently.

"Hey!" protested Michael, trying to pull the duvet back up.

"Nobody minds," said Jamie, pushing Michael away. "It's more comfortable like this." He was right. I threw back our duvet. Pete's hand was round my erection, my hand round his. Tony whistled. "Peter Parker, you're a well-built young man." Peter blushed but made no attempt to cover up.

"More," said Jamie.

"Listen," said Ackerley. "'Sex with males starts with kissing and touching. Maybe some games like strip poker or just, let's get these clothes off and down to business. There is kissing and fondling of breasts. Kissing and sucking the nipples and breasts, the navel, the penis, the balls, the ass. The 69 position is good, also lying on top of one another, kissing and thrusting our penises together. Having oral and anal sex. Nothing very far out or kinky.'"

"What's the 69 position?" asked Fletcher.

"That's what we were doing last night. Lying upside down. Sucking me, sucking you?"

"Isn't that an Abba song?" asked Fletcher.

"What?" Jamie sounded a trifle irritated.

"Sucking me, sucking you?...Ouch! That hurt!"

"It was meant to."

"What's really interesting," said Ackerley, "is what Shere Hite found out." The school's Headboy's powers of concentration were admirable. Honeyman had stripped off the bottom of Adrian's pyjamas; his fingers were embedded in the Sixth Former's crack.

"Hite found out that about forty percent of all boys have sex with each other. They toss each other off and it says here '36 per cent of boys also perform fellatio together.'"

"What's fellashi...?" asked Fletcher. "Have we done that?"

"Yes. It's only sucking each other's dicks," said Jamie.

"...and," continued Ackerley, "she found out that 'around twenty per cent have experienced anal penetration.'"

"Is that up the bum?" asked Fletcher.

"Yes," sighed Jamie.

"Oh, we've done that," said Michael brightly.

Adrian closed the book and laid it aside. "Truth or Dare," he said. He looked around the bed. "Truth. Put your hand up if you haven't done that."

Not a hand went up.

"Good for you," said Tony, looking with no little admiration at Peter. "That's fine then. We don't want any virgins in The Ram Stam Boys." He stripped off and pulled a naked Adrian the length of his body. "Let's celebrate."

The Shere Hite Report bounced around the bed as six naked boys celebrated.

* * *

We returned to school in triumph. Our prizes were already there. We were headlines in the local press. We were asked to do a number on local radio, and give interviews. Dr Honeyman was contacted by a musical agent but said everything was to be left until after Christmas. I was disappointed, but my disappointment vanished when Peter agreed to spend a week of the Christmas holidays at my home.

As our train pulled out of Kennet, I stood looking out of the carriage window, thinking what a brilliant term it had been. Peter stood behind me. I felt him press his erection into my crack. The Autumn term had been great; the Spring Term was going to be even better.

The Ram Stam Boys were on their way.

The End

© Copyright GLB Publishers by Chris Kent   1998

The entire Chris Kent Collection
is available only at GLB Publishers:

𝔗𝔥𝔢 𝔅𝔬𝔶𝔰 𝔬𝔣
𝔖𝔴𝔦𝔱𝔥𝔦𝔫𝔰 ℌ𝔞𝔩𝔩

1-879194-25-2

US $ 13.95

𝔅𝔬𝔶𝔰 𝔍𝔫
𝔖𝔥𝔬𝔯𝔱𝔰

1-879194-28-7

US $ 14.95

𝔗𝔥𝔢 ℜ𝔢𝔞𝔩
𝔗𝔬𝔪 𝔅𝔯𝔬𝔴𝔫'𝔰
𝔖𝔠𔥬𝔬𝔬𝔩 𝔇𝔞𝔶𝔰

1-879194-39-2

US $ 14.95

Boys Will
Be Boys:

Two Novellas

1-879194-40-6

US $ 14.95

Send check to:
GLB Publishers
P.O. Box 78212

San Francisco,
CA   94107

All Chris Kent books

are also available as

E-Books.

Each short story,

each novella, and

each novel

available separately at:

http://www.GLBpubs.com

Print them out on your own printer

in your choice of formats,

PDF (Adobe Reader)	Word
Text	Word Perfect
HTML	LIT (MS Reader)
RTF	MobiPocket

including the full color covers for your color printer.